I0570752

Totally Bound Publishing books by January Bain

THE TETRAD GROUP

RACING THE TIDE

JANUARY BAIN

Racing the Tide
ISBN # 978-1-83943-839-4
©Copyright January Bain 2018
Cover Art by Posh Gosh ©Copyright January 2018
Interior text design by Claire Siemaszkiewicz
Totally Bound Publishing

RACING
THE TIDE

Dedication

A huge vote of thanks, as always, to my amazing editor who always goes beyond the call of duty. And to my amazing husband, thank you for being you.

Chapter One

Day One: 5:13 a.m.

The bed trembled, its legs jerking and thudding about in a kind of macabre dance. Cole woke instantly. *Is this the big one?* The king-size bed shimmied and rattled a few more times, then settled back down, coming to rest slightly askew on the hardwood floor of his bedroom, the earth having released its rage. *Another fucking tremor.* He ran his hands through his sweat-damp hair, glancing over at the bedside table.

Five-fourteen a.m. He slid his gaze from the clock to the picture, as he did every morning, ready to administer his daily punishment. During the long night of sleeping intermittently, he had made up his mind, but now, looking at her face, he couldn't do it. He couldn't dishonor her memory in that way. *Especially not in that way. The coward's way.*

His mind zeroed in on the single event defining his life, the day haunting him every second the clock ticked. The day almost a year ago when he'd pulled into his driveway after a voice message he could make no sense of. Finding the front door ajar. Walking down a hallway so silent he could hear the pounding in his skull echoing his slamming pulse. Finding the bathroom door shut against him. One more obstacle. Turning the handle as slow as a swimmer in deep water, finding it unlocked, his throat tight and aching. The creak of the hinges. The door swung open. His vision darkening around the edges as he took in the horror of the scene. The heaviness in his chest that made him sink to the floor, gathering her into his arms. *No. Oh, God no. Not like this.*

His cell phone rang in the dead stillness of a house that had once been a home, jerking him back into the present. Swallowing hard, he picked up the phone from the table, turning his back on the photo of his wife and himself mugging for the camera in happier times. The words of his father haunted him. '*A real man never cries, son, no matter what*'. Did he mean even if the worst thing that could happen, happened?

"Yeah." He managed one sharp word.

"Hey, Cole, it's Jake. How's it going?"

Hearing his friend's voice ratcheted down his anxiety, put the cap back on his demons. Had it been only nine months ago that they had put Kastrati and his son away for crimes against humanity? The one bright spot in the past year had been the whirlwind operation involving Jake and his new wife, Silk. Teaming up, they had been successful in putting the Kastrati crew, a cartel that had been on his radar for some time, behind bars for trafficking in women and drugs.

Silk had borne the worst of it, when the son's senseless drunk-driving had left her sister and her sister's unborn child dead on the streets of LA. She'd even gone after the man herself when he'd been released on a technicality with the help of high-priced lawyers—she'd been waiting with a high-powered rifle across from the courthouse to take him down. And that was how she and Jake had met. Better than a dating agency, Cole supposed. A more awesome and skilled pair of operatives he could not hope to meet. Jake with his brilliant and fine-tuned military skills and Silk with her PI's investigative knowledge and dedication. She was almost as obsessive as he was about taking out the bad guys.

When he didn't answer right away, Jake asked with a hint of concern in his voice, "Did I wake you?"

"No. A fucking tremor managed to do that this morning. Seems the San Andreas fault is unhappy these days. Playing with us mortals and reminding everyone who's the boss. Other than that—I'm fine. How's the new family?"

He cleared his throat and focused on the present. He got up and padded into the living room to open the drapes, staring out at a world that appeared normal, on the surface, anyway. He knew better. A dark abyss lurked underneath, just waiting to swallow a person whole. *Not going to happen. Life is precious, even when crawling through hell.* Staying there kept Mathew's memory intact and he'd not give that up for anything. Someone had to remember his little boy. *Keep him alive.* And someone had to try to save others. Do what they could. *Choose me.*

"Great. Glad you're okay. We were wondering if you've got the time to come our way for a visit?"

"Sure, what's up?" He recognized Silk's excited voice in the background as she insisted, "Just ask him already!"

Now, it was Jake's turn to clear his throat. What was making his friend who had undergone the horrors of war nervous? "I had intended to wait until you got here, but you know our Silky. Well, here it goes. So, we're in the process of starting up our own company — The TETRAD Group. I think it could be right up your alley, Cole, with your need to rush in and rescue others, not to mention that your skills and abilities complement Silk's and mine perfectly. You know we shone as a team when we worked together to take down the Kastrati crew a few months back. Silk and I still talk about it all the time, thinking — hell yeah, we can do more. All of us, together, taking on cases for people who have nowhere else to turn. We can go and do things even law enforcement can't and yet have their support and insight because Quinn Malone's already on board with his far-reaching connections. I know you've worked with him lots in the past. He can bring a slew of abilities to the group, what with his undercover operative skills from working as a FBI agent and his former career as a lawyer. He knows the law inside and out, just like you do. Isn't that where you met? At law school?"

"Yeah, Quinn and I competed for top honors in our graduating class." *A long time ago and in a land far away.*

"What do you say, buddy, want to come to Vancouver and discuss it? Become one of the four founding members? Our aim is to help people who have trouble going to the local authorities — you know — do whatever it takes to make a difference and protect the innocent. Like you've been doing already. But with your tech savvy, hacking skills, undercover experience and understanding of the human mind, we would be unstoppable. Strength in numbers with a diverse range of overlapping skills brought into the mix from all of us. We'll stand together, strong and proud.

Make a difference in this world that's desperate for more heroes."

Do I? Maybe this is what I need. A complete change. And working together on cases meant so much more could be done. He had an admiration for the like-minded, married pair of Jake and Silk. And he'd worked off and on with Quinn over the past few years, his contact with the former FBI agent proving invaluable to his own personal crusades when he'd used up every bit of knowledge he could throw at criminals allowed by law, and then some.

The guy was the best. Knew how to play the dual role of human being and undercover agent and not mix up the two. He always got which side of the law he was on. Cole understood first-hand how hard that could be, acting at being one of them without becoming one of them. Learning to live with duality. It was hard enough infiltrating a motorcycle club or a drug cartel, but when he'd taken it to a far more disgusting level to get close to the nefarious perverts of NAMBLA, the North American Man-Boy Love Association, and had to listen to their sickening conversations and self-justifications, well, that took it to a level Cole found he was unable to deal with, though Quinn had gone on a righteous crusade and brought the fuckers down. Even having to talk Cole off a ledge when he'd threatened to blow up the convention center where the group was holding one of its secret annual meetings. Cole had to admire not only his dedication, but his loyalty to the cause and to friends.

Hell, Quinn even had a sense of humor about his undercover work, sending one criminal to jail when he was posing as a drug dealer and having the asshole call him from there to ask him to "raise bail". He'd done that all right. Raised it to a million with the help of

11

inside officials—not quite what the creep had meant. Though the time when Cole had posed as a hitman-for-hire in an online sting to take down a dirty lawyer looking for a revenge killing on a business partner and his innocent wife—that time had cemented the loyalty of their friendship when Quinn had smoothed things over with law enforcement. Things have a way of going awry when Cole worked a case driven by emotion, lack of sleep and an intense drive for justice. No apologies. *It's who I am.*

People said they looked alike, but Cole could never see it, at least not anymore since he'd lost so much weight and Quinn now outweighed him by a good twenty pounds. Sure, they both had dark, military-short hair and brown eyes, but that was where the similarity ended. Besides, his nose had been broken playing basketball—being so big and tall had made Cole a favorite on his college team. *God, those were simpler days.*

In a blink of an eye, the series of cases they'd been involved in flashed through his mind, pushing him to a quick decision.

"Sure. What the hell. I'll come up, see how things work out on a trial basis. Not much going on right now, anyway. Kind of between things. I can close up shop for a few days and not a soul would know I'm gone." He shrugged, staring out of his front window at a neighbor now watering his lawn. "I'll catch a plane tomorrow and text you the time."

"Great! That's great." The palpable relief in his friend's voice was nice to hear. Made him feel needed, something he'd not experienced for a long while. He ended the call and strode into his office, where he booted up his laptop to check out airline reservations.

He found a flight with a layover in Denver and booked it. *God, I need coffee.*

His phone rang again. *So much for coffee.*

"Cole," Jon said before he could even say hello, the hard edge to his friend's tone unusual. *Hmm. What now?*

"Hey, Jon, I was just thinking about you. Great minds think alike. Just planning on calling you about dropping by and visiting tomorrow. I have a layover in Denver planned." Jon lived in Denver, had for the past fifteen years, since his daughter Sara's birth, his and Rose's only child. "How you doing?"

"Been better, but it'll be good to see you. How about you? How you holding up?"

"I'm okay. What's up with you?" A tightening of his stomach muscles made Cole straighten in his chair, all senses alert. He shut his laptop lid and homed in on the voice coming over the phone, paying careful attention to each nuance. In the psychology courses he'd taken, he'd discovered the subtle clues for what a human being wanted to share or tell a listener were there, not hidden at all.

"Sorry, it's just business. So much going on right now. Crazy busy — you know how it is. But you're going to be here soon, so we can talk then."

It was damn well more than just business. But it was also obvious Jon would never say whatever was troubling him over the phone. Cole would get to the bottom of it tomorrow, that was for damn sure.

"I'm okay. Got an interesting job offer I'll tell you about also, if you're sure you have the time?"

"Sure, we'd love to see you. You know how Rose dotes on you." Jon's voice softened, sounding more himself, when he spoke of his wife. A good woman, Rose. Cole swallowed hard, regret riding him hard.

"Okay, tomorrow it is."

Cole hung up the phone, his nerves on edge. He went into the galley kitchen, filling a cup with instant coffee and adding hot water from the special machine that kept water hot or cold all the time. He drank it standing over the kitchen sink, surveying his neglected backyard that had used to be his pride and joy. The bright red swing set he'd sweated over a few years ago needed a coat of paint, its rusty surface beginning to lean. *Yes. Past time to move on and do more.*

* * * *

Day Two: 3:23 p.m.

Cole threw his bag into the back of the taxi, settling into the passenger side.

"Where can I take you?"

He gave the driver Jon's address on Circle Drive in the gated and historic Country Club neighborhood of Denver. Why were they meeting at his home and not at the office? Jon was president of a huge tech giant and never took time off. How else could a man born without family money afford one of the finest mansions in all of Denver?

"No traffic, so we'll be there in forty minutes or so. Nice part of town," the driver added, giving him a speculative look. Had the cost of the trip just gone up? The idea grated on Cole. Another part of him advised not to make a mountain out of a molehill. Principle won out yet again.

"Ever read *The Art of War* by Sin Tzu?"

"No, why?"

"The passage, 'the skillful soldier does not raise a second levy' comes to mind."

"What's that supposed to mean?" The middle-aged driver's head turned around on his thick neck as he gave Cole a belligerent look. "You think I'm going to cheat you, is that it?" His face reddened, his eyes narrowing with anger.

"Just sayin' I'm prepared to give you a generous tip." Cole tried to smooth the waters, unsure of just when he had become this testy. *What's the matter with me? Just a guy trying to make a decent living driving a taxi, for Christ's sake.* He shook his head. He needed to get his sense of humor unearthed. "Sorry, it's been a bad year."

"Yeah, we all have those, buddy. No need to insult others." The guy settled down, Cole observed glancing in the rearview mirror, though the red patches remained on his chubby cheeks that bristled with a day or two's growth of salt-and-pepper whiskers.

"I said I'm sorry."

"Okay, then. Let's forget it."

The man remained silent all the way to Jon's, making Cole feel the double lash of guilt and regret. No matter what waited for him in Canada, it could not be worse than what he had been living these past months.

He straightened in his seat as the driver pulled into the curving driveway with the English gardens standing proud in an oasis of breathtaking grandeur nestled between the entrance and exit. *Focus on right now, feel the earth beneath you and breathe deeply.* He reminded himself of the mantra recommended by a website for those experiencing moments of stress. Too bad they didn't have something to improve his disposition, as well. He always did better when he had something important to focus on. He prayed there would be lots of action in Vancouver—that was, if he took the job.

He over-tipped the guy, hauled out his duffel bag from the back seat and watched the yellow taxi spin its wheels getting away.

Okay. A visit with an old friend might improve his mood. He thought over Jon's eclectic interests—everything from computers to fine art. Their university days had sunk the roots deep for a solid friendship based on sharing an unquenchable thirst for knowledge, information and research. A rare commodity, he'd since discovered.

He ventured up to the front door and rang the bell. A cat joined him on the top step, rubbing against his pant leg. He leaned down and patted its sleek coal-black head, scratching behind its ears as it reared up against him, purring loudly. "Hey, boy, you looking to get in, too?" he asked just as the door opened. The cat skirted around Jon and into the house, making his friend look down.

"Hey, Jon, good to see you. Hope he's a friend of yours?"

His friend's head came back up and his tired, worried eyes met Cole's. Cole had meant the cat, but it took a moment for the question to register with Jon. Cole could see it in his slow reaction time. What was wrong? His gut tightened. It was not the norm either for Jon to answer the doorbell and an eerie quiet in the dark hallway behind him gave the sense no one else was home. The Sterling household tended to bustle with activity—his daughter, Sara, filling it with her many friends, much encouraged by her doting father. It had made it hard for Cole this past year to visit the family, though, he never would say so. His friend deserved his happiness.

"Hey, Cole. Yeah, Teako San belongs with us."

The two men hugged, an awkward moment, before pulling apart. Jon looked unkempt, not his usual well-groomed self, even giving off a slight pungent smell, so unlike his friend. Cole breathed deep, recognizing it. *Fear. Oh, God.*

"What's wrong?" he asked, all his senses on high alert. He rubbed the back of his neck in an effort to ease the tension.

"Nothing."

"Don't give me that. This is me you're talking to. I know you too well. Something's wrong and it's not just you working too hard. You've always done that. I warn you, I'm not leaving here until you tell me what it is."

Jon ran a shaky hand through his hair that had gone grey almost overnight, pushing the thick waves back from his face, then pinching the skin on his throat, drawing his dark eyebrows together. He didn't look Cole in the eye, but kept his glance flitting around the room, as if he were looking for something. Cole's gut tightened. He'd never seen his friend so distracted. At Yale, Jon had been the guy he'd have voted for never losing his cool. Or his witty sense of humor. Many a night had been spent playing poker, drinking beer and joking around, trying to out-do the other's outrageous remarks. Studious they might have been, monks never.

"Come in. We can talk inside."

Cole dropped his bag onto the black and white chess-patterned marble floor in the foyer and turned to follow Jon, who was beckoning him down the hallway.

"I don't want Rose to be disturbed. She's resting, not feeling well," he said by way of explanation as he preceded Cole into the study, heading straight for the bar set up near his desk. His laptop stood open on the desktop, amid a jumbled mess of paper, and an ashtray half-filled with cigarette butts completed the odd picture. Maybe Jon wasn't the neatest guy in the world, but his wife would never have sanctioned this. If she had taken to her bed, it made some sense, at least. Maybe Jon was worried about her health?

"I'm sorry about Rose not feeling well. Please give her my sympathy."

"Thanks. Want a drink?" Jon poured himself a stiff whiskey from the array of crystal decanters laid out on the cart with its fancy globe-like lid rolled back to expose the contents. His friend had always had great taste, preferring to buy something only once and of the best quality, even in university. The same philosophy Cole applied to his tech acquisitions, but not so much in his private life, at least not anymore. He couldn't remember the last time he'd bought something new, something that gave him more than a second of satisfaction, except for the tools of his trade.

"The same poison and add some water, thanks." He kept himself from remarking on the time of day and just accepted the glass handed him, observing for the hundredth time the excellent rendition of Salvador Dali's *The Persistence of Memory*, on the wall. Jon had once told him that he'd bought it not because of the investment—it was the only one in his home not an original piece of work and banished by his wife to his own space in any home they'd occupied—but because it spoke to him on another level.

The concept of time and how it could be manipulated and managed fascinated his friend. And Cole had to admit, it intrigued him, as well, though, the artist had always insisted he hadn't painted it with thoughts of Einstein's theory of relativity in mind, but rather with the idea of a camembert melting in the sun. Every time he viewed the famous painting, Cole found himself fascinated by the same thought—would time ever prove to be truly malleable by humans? Even today, with dark worries pressing in on all sides, he felt its energy.

"I should give you that painting," Jon said. "Rose hates it. Says it lacks continuity and goes against the Chinese tradition of art. I just think it's because we didn't buy it together."

Cole shrugged, not used to Jon criticizing his wife, who had spoken his wedding vows stating the sun and the stars rose and set upon her, and, until now, nothing in his actions disproving the truth of his words. "I like it because it makes me think outside the box."

Jon grunted and took another large swig of his whiskey, turning away from the print and slumping down into his office chair.

"Have a seat." Jon gestured at another chair by his side.

"I didn't know you'd taken up smoking again." Cole kept his voice noncommittal as he sat. Jon had given up the vice at university when he'd met Rose.

"Rose doesn't know, but I've never been able to give it up entirely. Kind of got out of hand last night, I guess. I'd better flush the butts before she sees." Jon looked around as if spying the desk top mess for the first time.

Cole's gut tightened further, his mouth going dry. "So, spill it." Cole took a swallow of his drink, winced slightly at the strength of the whiskey lacking enough water and set it down between two stacks of papers. He needed to keep his wits about him, thirsty or not.

Jon took a deep breath, his eyes focused on the computer screen. "I didn't want to share this, especially with you—God knows it's not right, considering all you've been through. It's bad, Cole, and I'm worried it might be best to keep you right the hell out of it. It's not fair to you. I shouldn't have called you. I don't want to cause you any more pain."

"Fuck. Just show me. I won't leave here until you do, anyway," Cole threatened. Nothing was worse than not knowing.

"Okay. But you need to prepare yourself. Here—read it." He turned the laptop to make it easier for Cole, his misgivings clear on his face.

The short hairs on the back of Cole's neck sprang into action as he read the terse message. And his stomach dropped to the floor, filling with the heavy weight of dread that only a man who had been through what he had could know or understand.

Phone this number at exactly seven a.m.

A phone number followed and a photo of Jon's daughter Sara was attached. Her white prom dress soiled and torn and her dark hair disheveled, she looked frightened, her eyes wide and staring at whoever was snapping the picture. The background was blurry, giving away nothing about the location.

"What the hell? When did this arrive? What was she doing last night?"

"Last night. After midnight. She'd gone to her prom. I thought she was safe—she went with her usual group of friends. I thought she was too young, but Rose insisted it would be okay going with a group of friends, rather than a date. But you know kids, talking it up online. Everyone knew about the event. She looked so pretty when she left in her gown—like an angel. My God, what's going to happen to her?" Jon's face turned horrified once again. Cole had to keep him focused. Get every detail out of him.

"You've located the source? And called the number? Brought in anybody else? Authorities of any kind?" Cole shot off the questions. *Don't think of anything else. Just focus. Get the answers.*

Jon nodded, regaining control as he relayed the facts. "Yes. I recorded the phone call. Burner phone was used. Impossible to trace. I haven't located the location yet of the email — it's been bounced all over the damn place. And I haven't called the authorities — not yet, anyway. What are they going to do? They can't write the damn code."

"What code?" Cole demanded.

Jon made a couple of key strokes on the laptop and a strange voice began speaking with a slight Asian accent, his tone business-like and serious. He spoke the words with perfect enunciation, the speech either written down or memorized.

"I think you can see by the attachment that we are involved in a very serious undertaking. We have a business proposition for you and your company that will be very profitable for all of us long-term. We require you to write a computer software program that's undetectable and will drain bitcoins from every wallet from every company worldwide and relocate them to an account that will be provided. You have five days if you wish to see your daughter alive again. Sara is safe for now at a foreign location where it is — I promise — impossible to find her. Not even if you had months of lead time could you hope to do so. I suggest it would be far better to spend your energies on doing what we ask than trying to find the needle in the haystack. Be warned. We are watching you, your house, and know everything being said. Do not go to the authorities if you want to see your daughter again. You have five days. The clock is ticking. Use the time wisely. Otherwise, what happens to Sara will be out of our control. We will be in touch."

"That's impossible—" Jon's voice began speaking over the phone, but a loud click could be heard over the recording as the person hung up.

"Christ, what a clusterfuck." Cole pursed his lips, narrowing his eyes in thought, feeling as though he'd been punched in the stomach by a giantslayer. He had to keep it together for his friend's sake, though, the situation sickened him to the core and could throw him back into the deepest pit of hell if he let it. He knew that place all too well. The acid pain that lashed and burned a soul with endless torment until time became a second-to-second battle just to stay alive. To draw one more breath. He knew it because he'd spent endless months there. *In living hell.* No. He had to hold on, believe he could help in some way. "Let me have a look at this. Have you discovered the source?"

"Christ!" Jon rubbed at his forehead, his agitation clear. "I've been so busy working on the bitcoin solution, I've neglected the *fucking* obvious."

Jon pushed the computer closer to him, his eyes dark with a bottomless anguish. Cole began searching the operating system to follow the breadcrumbs left by the email, making himself focus only on what could be done in the moment and not the dark past. Nothing was hidden. Not when he knew where to look. Not even on the dark web, the illegal underground web that threatened to steal lives and souls.

"Aha, here we go." Cole frowned at the black and white screen filled with scrolling strings of source code, forcing him to focus. "The damn thing originated from an IP address in Vancouver. Can you believe it? I'm headed there now."

Cole turned to his friend. "Can you do this thing that's being asked? Have you got the resources? The programmers to hack into either the original program or into one of the companies providing the service?"

"I don't see how this can be done, though, that's all I've been working on, even with my bank of supercomputers. The original program is nearly flawless. Only been tampered with once. August 11, 2013, when a bug in a pseudorandom number generator within the Android operating system was exploited to steal from wallets generated by the apps. It was patched within forty-eight hours. Far, far easier to hack into a service provider. It's been done numerous times already. But that's not what the guy is asking for. He wants a drain on the original system, not a hack that can be discovered. He's thinking bigger and longer-term than that, but fuck, five days—it's not possible in the slightest."

Jon shook his head, his expression bleaker if possible. He raised a trembling hand to pinch at the skin on his throat. "I'm not certain it even can be done. Their dual public and private key cryptography and advanced mathematics were designed specifically to prevent it."

Cole held his tongue. Should he share what he knew? Or would it only offer false hope if he couldn't pull it off? No. *I can do this, goddamn it. Somehow. No other child dies on my watch.*

"I might know someone," he began, ignoring the bell ringing in the back of his mind, telling him he was venturing into difficult territory. Unknown territory that could come back and bite him on the ass remembering how vehement 'Satoshi' was about not ever being coerced for *any* reason, *ever* again into getting involved with the shit politics and policies of the underground network, remembering the exact words he'd used on his last visit, which seemed a lifetime ago. But his friend was screaming for help, no matter how slim it was, he had to offer hope.

"Who? Fuck. Spill it. Anything. If you know anyone that can help — please, please, say, for the love of God. I need help, Cole."

"The ghost behind the original program who washed his hands of the whole operation a few years back. Felt his vision was being exploited by the institutions he had built the program to keep out. The guy's obsessed with the ideology of how the balance of power between corporations and governments one hand and the individual on the other is essential to maintain a free society. A strict hardliner who wants big business out of the process of gathering and selling info on the individual. Too idealistic for this world, though I admire his attempt at a utopian society."

"Mr. Satoshi Nakamoto? You know who he is?" Jon sat up straight in his chair as he comprehended the magnitude of the information. No one in the free world was known to have the identity of the man responsible for bitcoins. Journalists had long speculated on his identity and even the country of his origin.

"This is in the strictest confidence, but yes, we go way back."

"Oh, my God, that's — I don't know what to say."

"I can't promise you anything, but I will try, you have my word."

"Please, anything, tell him anything I have is his if he will help my little girl! She's so innocent — I never thought anything like this could happen." Jon's eyes filled with unshed tears and he turned away, his shoulders shaking as he struggled to keep his emotions in check.

Cole cleared his throat. "In the meantime, something else fortuitous is in the works. I've been offered a partnership in Vancouver by a man starting up a new company, the TETRAD Group, and I think helping Sara is something they're going to want to be in on. Their mandate is to help those unable to go to the authorities. And if this doesn't count, I don't know what does."

Jon got up and strode over to the bar and poured a glass of water from a crystal decanter, his expression thoughtful.

"I'd like one, as well," Cole said.

"Yes, of course. Or maybe coffee?"

"I thought you'd never ask," he said.

"You should talk. At university, you could drink the best of us under the table."

Thank God. His friend was back. Now, he had to pray that this thing could be done. *Five days. Fuck.* It sounded damn near impossible to him as well, but he'd never let Jon know that or ever give up. Sara was coming home no matter what it took. He'd get down on his hands and knees and beg 'Satoshi' if he had to.

* * * *

"You a rat?" Uncle Chang demanded, a well-thumbed book held open, a forefinger marking his spot on the page. He glanced up from studying it to bore his gaze into the young man seated across from him.

Tommy's head swiveled halfway around on his scrawny neck, his dark eyes widening as the older man locked glances with him. Uncle's constant blank stare gave nothing away. In the back of the café that bore his uncle's name, Tommy's full attention had been focused on the new waitress gliding between the small group of tables, making the unexpected question a jarring force throwing him far out of his comfort zone. He swallowed, hard, the action visible in his bobbing Adam's apple as he tugged at his few chin whiskers. Still, it was very satisfying that his whiskers were black, seeing how gray Uncle's had turned in the past year, though his hair was still black, combed straight back from his high forehead and sharp cheekbones. *Getting on, old man.*

"What? Me? A rat?" Sweat trickled from his armpits, soaking his black T-shirt. He always wore black. As a member of the BTK, short for Born to Kill, it seemed a wise choice. *Black hides bloodstains.*

"Yeah, you born in 1996, right? Year of the Yang Fire Rat. Makes you ambitious, hard-working and thrifty, with very good intuition. This is your year — if you don't fuck it up. Phttttt — " Uncle slowly shook his head at the great tragedy. "The young today. Wasted. Think all those fancy gadgets make them something. Think you can buy the answers. Makes you idiot if you let everyone know your business."

Tommy's stomach rolled once and settled. Uncle gave nothing away, though Tommy suspected the man knew all too well what he was doing. He forgot the waitress, instead giving his uncle his full attention. His uncle might be stuck in the past, with his money laundering and skin trade and his foolish dislike of all things technological. He even insisted on still doing all business face-to-face! But, Uncle's name carried serious weight in Chinatown and without the family connection, Tommy understood he would be cut out of the business. Yes, he needed to keep Uncle onboard, had to demonstrate his own goodwill now more than ever, working at keeping the excitement from showing on his face as he recalled the recent phone call with its potential to change his life. *Could be my golden ticket.*

Then we'll see how much technology sucks. Make me a lion, not a rat, old man.

The man on the phone had wanted younger, newer ideas, telling Tommy that he'd heard he was the brightest star in his uncle's organization. Yes, he had many big ideas, thinking how often he'd been stymied by his stuck-in-the-past uncle, his thoughts shut down before he even got a fair say. *Not right.* The man on the phone had been so full of encouragement, too, telling Tommy he could go far, far as he wanted with *his* backing. His stomach twitched with excitement. One day, maybe soon, Tommy would be the big man in Chinatown. The one everyone came to, heads bowed with respect. In the meantime, he had to be careful, just as the guy had cautioned. Had to be seen to do what Uncle wanted. *Outsmart Confucius.* Even if it sucked.

"I got an important job for a fire rat who can handle himself." Uncle closed the cover of his book and set it aside and took a sip of his green tea from the fragile china cup, his claw-like hands tightening around it.

Tommy nodded, not trusting himself to speak.

Chapter Two

Day Two: 8:51 p.m.

The sexy beat of Dwight Yoakam's version of *Honky-Tonk Man* wormed its way through Gabrielle Banks' body, making her tap her red cowgirl-booted toes on the wide-planked floor. She'd chosen the small round table in the Legend Saloon on purpose for easy viewing of the entire space, keeping a keen eye out for new arrivals. She scanned the Friday-night crowd for the umpteenth time, impatient for the expected guy to arrive. A segment of the bar's clientele had lined up to one side, busy egging one another on to ride the mechanical bull. Line dancing was about to begin and she'd hoped to escape before then.

She ran her hand over her long honey-brown hair in its ponytail, smoothing a few wayward tendrils back from her face, wishing yet again she'd been blessed with more height. But she was satisfied with a couple of gifts she had inherited from her beautiful mama, that was, her well-endowed curves and her pretty face, because both of them made her job of tricking men into thinking she was available and just *had* to have them a whole lot easier. She tried for a better view, sitting up straighter in the chair. At least the music didn't suck like the last bar she'd been forced to hang out in trying to catch the cheating husband in his finest moment.

"Want another?" Celine asked. Her decoy friend for the evening and younger sister by all of eleven months and three days gestured, signaling the waitress.

"Nah, I don't think he's going to show, anyway." She'd been doing this for the past three nights running—sitting and waiting for Mr. My-wife-is-not-enough-for-me Smith to make his appearance, looking for a little action. Yeah, his name was Smith, George Smith, and his soon-to-be-ex-wife was looking to cut his balls off. In financial terms, that was. One taped video of him hitting on her or someone else in the bar, one incriminating moment to begin divorce proceedings saved on her phone, and she was out of there.

She'd been stuck with too many of these kinds of cases this past year in an effort to make a dint in her ex's gambling debts. Ah, yes. Her ex. aka the lying cheating skunk who'd fled the country, leaving her in the soup. Why had she hooked up with a con man who ran a casino, again? Oh, yeah, that charming I-can't-live-without-you persona had hidden his true nature. A coward who'd deserted her the moment it was discovered he wouldn't be able to repay his mounting debts, leaving her to face the loan sharks—alone. She'd worked out a repayment plan—well, it had either been that or they'd break some part of her, and she was partial to all her limbs, thank you very much. If she was lucky, she'd be finished with the pay-off about the same time as she was due to retire.

Think about something else. Okay, back to her usual beef. Did every man cheat on his wife? Seemed that way some nights as she watched the antics in the different bars and clubs she frequented to make a living. Last night's experience still rankled, that asshole who'd thought *No* was just a preliminary for a future *Yes.* As though she was blind and couldn't see the white strip of skin on his left hand where his wedding ring had resided not fifteen minutes earlier. *Drunken, stupid assholes.*

But the worst one of all, the one who still stuck like a burr, that creep from that religious sect she'd decided to go after all on her own, for free, when she'd found out about him through a colleague. The one who thought he was God's gift to the world and should fill his house with all their worldly goods. Bastard, taking advantage of men and women alike, and expecting others to turn a blind eye just because he had what he thought of as religious sanction to build his dirty game upon. *Fuck, not on my watch is he going to get away with it.*

She came back to the present with a lurch of consciousness, Celine vying for her attention, tugging at her arm.

"Hey, you in there or in La La Land? Just one more, sis, okay? I need a little more time to catch that new guy's eye," Celine stage-whispered in her ear. She nodded in the direction of a man striding toward them. He sat at an empty table less than eight feet away. *Hmm.* He looked like the kind of guy who thought he was every woman's fantasy, his polished yet scruffy appearance a ploy at pretending he didn't care. She'd bet he used one of those special razors that kept his beard that precise length. No one was *that* good-looking without doing a little something.

A big, wide-shouldered man, he wasn't dressed like the rest of the patrons, having opted for a black T-shirt and faded blue jeans. He spoke to the waitress in a gravelly voice, asking about takeout, and she handed him a menu. He glanced over, checking both of them out then coming back to lock eyes with her for that split second that men and women share in bars.

Only this time, the effect was paralyzing. His eyes were whiskey-brown and shadowed. And they were hard. Flint hard. Every line of muscle in his handsome face was tight and tense. *Worry or something more disturbing?* The corner of his mouth twitched into a semblance of a smile that didn't reached his eyes. The air between them crackled with tension like a direct hit from a lightning bolt. *What the hell?* Her lips parting, she took a sharp intake of breath, steadying herself. Then he looked away, breaking eye contact. She swallowed hard. *Whoa. What just happened?*

"What? That pretty boy?" Gabby said, whispering into her sister's ear, pretending indifference. She twisted in the chair, facing another direction. She'd seen way too much of what men were capable to ever fall for someone who looked that full of himself. Or that good.

"Yeah. Well, at least I'm open for business, Gabrielle." Celine used her sister's full name for emphasis, annoying her further, though, Celine did keep her voice low enough not to be overheard. Thank the heavens. "Remember the warning in *Booty Call* — you know — the one about cobwebs? I'd be more worrying about its best-before date." Celine chuckled, her expression smug, scoring a direct hit.

Gabby blushed, the jab getting under her skin. She hissed, "It's not a quart of milk — it won't go off, for heaven's sake!" She scanned the bar, careful not to lock eyes with the man again. Never again. Must be the haunting lyrics of the song *A Thousand Miles from Nowhere* now playing on the jukebox and the terrible longing that always overcame her when she heard it that had temporarily hijacked her brain. That was it. "I've got too much self-respect to let a guy like that get in my pants. He'd expect me to do all the heavy lifting."

"Huh," Celine snorted, forgetting to be quiet. "Just 'cause he's pretty doesn't mean he doesn't know how to go downtown." She wiggled her well arched brows for emphasis, tucking her long honey-brown hair behind her ears, her baby-blue eyes with their golden specks feigning innocence. If Gabby ever needed to know what she'd would look like if she took the best care of her appearance and let her hair down once in a while, all she had to do was check out her baby sister. They teased each other over which one of them might be an actual Doppelgänger. Not funny, but quite useful applied to the correct situation. "And furthermore, I find —"

Gabby held up a hand to block further discussion. "I don't want to hear it, okay? I'll get us another round of drinks, but that's it. All my budget can handle. The prices in this place are outrageous. And I already sprang for nachos and pulled pork. Going to be paying for that indulgence tomorrow, guaranteed. Wallet *and* waistline."

This earned her a second snort, more pronounced than the first.

"Hang on, just got a text." Gabby read the short message, her stomach tightening, feeling bad for the woman wanting to know if her husband had shown up yet. And to tell her she had a referral for her, another woman certain her working-all-the time husband was cheating on her. Love sucked.

"What is it?"

"Got another job. And just in time. Between food and drink these past three nights, my expense account is running on empty." Gabby took a deep breath, about to read it aloud, but a poke in the ribs made her glance up.

"Look, isn't that your guy? Your client's husband? And check out who's on his arm. Think that's a coincidence?" Celine asked, her stage-whisper more gleeful than quiet.

"Shush, we're undercover here. And no, I don't believe in coincidences. Everything happens for a reason." *Maybe I won't have to be the honey trap after all, getting him to spend time alone with me.*

"Like I don't know that. But, see, buying me pulled pork and dirty martinis is good luck for you. Guy shows up and you get another job."

The alleged cheater and his companion disappeared, choosing one of the few intimate booths available. Not too dumb. Harder to catch him at it. But not impossible, of course. At least she wouldn't have to put up with him hitting on her. And to think he had such an attractive wife and two adorable toddlers waiting at home. Mattie and Connor, four and two. Why, just yesterday she'd played with them as their mother had poured her heart out, Connor crawling up on her lap with his red fire engine and dimpled, chubby cheeks she just had to kiss. The deadbeat in the bar must have promised to be true to Ashley at some time, right? Hell, they'd only been married for five years. But no, here he was breaking his wedding vows as easy as apple pie, well before the supposed seven-year itch. *No guy is ever going to get that chance with me. Shut him down first.*

"Ladies and gents, it's line-dancing time! Cozy up and choose your partner."

The female under scrutiny stood and Gabby did as well. She avoided looking anywhere else, following the young woman to the room marked *Cowgirls*. Someone had written in black marker under the sign since she'd last been there. It now said *Cougars Welcome*.

She took out her phone, snapped a photo of the altered sign just for the hell of it, pushed open the bathroom door and began to play a mindless game on her phone as the woman used one of the stalls.

Gabby tapped her toes, waiting for the young woman to emerge. She did, neglected to wash her hands—yuck—and swanned out. Gabby sighed, washed her own hands and dried them under a blast of sizzling air.

She followed the female, making sure to pass the booth, checking out Mr. All-Wrong. He kissed the new arrival, planted another one on her neck and nuzzled her for good measure, making her smile and giggle as he draped his arm around her. He let it dangle low enough to cop a feel of a breast. *Grrr. So disgusting.* They deserved each other. She pretended to stumble from a short distance away, preparing to bring the phone up to snap a quick photo, before grasping the table edge to keep from tumbling to the floor. Classic move well-practiced. She just needed good follow-through.

But a strong pair of hands grasped hold of her, preventing her from enacting the entire pantomime, and, worse, knocking her phone from her hand to the floor in the brouhaha.

"What the fuck!" she exclaimed, trying to pull away from the interference. *Oh, God, not him.* In a state of shock, she looked up at him, forgetting she wanted to get away. It was that guy, the one she'd locked glances with earlier. He must have come in just to order takeout. And that food now lay strewn on the floor, bag torn and contents looking less than appetizing.

"You all right?" he grunted, his growly voice resonating and tugging on a sympathetic chord deep inside, all the way to her down to her quaking core, and still he held onto her, didn't let her go. A wild urge to rub up against his hard body nearly overcame her. *Good Lord. What the fuck is the matter with me?*

"I'm fine." She managed to squeak out the words and added a scowl, remembering after an extended interlude to pull out of his embrace. She avoided looking in his eyes. His hands were warm and strong as he held her firmly around the waist before releasing her, brushing a breast that had all at once acquired a sensitive peak. His touch was commanding, electrifying. She swallowed then glanced at the floor, surveying the quick-congealing mess as she gathered up her strewn facilities, wishing they could have stayed pressed together for a whole lot longer. "But I'm afraid your food took a direct hit."

"Damn, I wanted to treat them on my first night in town." The man shook his head, giving the floor a disgusted look. "I'll need to reorder."

"I should pay for it," she offered, feeling guilty, warmth creeping up her spine. Was he married? She dared a glance and their eyes locked. *Again. Oh, good grief.* Her physical body found him dreamy as hell while her mental state fought back, battling away at the suggestion of even an atom's worth of attraction. Failed. *Pheromones are a pain in the ass.* She took a deep breath. Hot cinnamon shot through with a healthy dose of testosterone tantalized her nostrils, sending her into sensory overload in a flash.

"No need." He bent down, giving a great view of his ass as his jeans pulled tight. When he stood back up, she dared a look at his package. Regretted it. Well-endowed didn't even begin to cover it. Her blood sizzled with anticipation and she overheated. Damn it, now she'd be red in the face. "Your phone looks okay." He handed it to her and their fingers touched. She jumped back from the static spark that jumped between them, laughing nervously.

"The air must be dry," she said. Too witty for words.

"Must be," he said.

"Well, if you're sure about the food, I'll get back to my sister."

"Yeah, I'm sure. No problem." His tone had a lyrical southern charm she found intriguing. She loved placing accents. And his sounded so much nicer than her boring old Canadian one. Beige, the color of Canada, in her opinion, and the national choice for all home decorating. Well, that might be a small exaggeration, but she'd seen enough beige to last a lifetime. She wanted color, craved it in her life. And knew she couldn't afford color. Not now, not ever. But a gal could dream, right? This guy gave off waves of off-beat color and heat—maybe that was why the instant lust alert? She shivered, her body inundated with sensations.

"Texas, right?"

"Excuse me?"

"Where you came from. Your accent."

"Yes, Houston originally. Been living in LA the past few years."

"'He rides from Texas on a big white horse'," she recited the lyrics, teasing him. When his expression shifted to one that looked like he was considering her certifiable, she added. "Beach Boys—*Long, Tall Texan*. Remember?" When he said nothing, she asked, "Here on business?" When was the last time she'd been this nervous around a man? In her experience most were lying, cheating bastards undeserving of even the slightest bit of attention.

"Yeah, well, I guess I should get going. My friends are waiting for their dinner. I wanted to treat them, tonight being my first night in town and all."

Yeah, you said that already. Maybe he was as discombobulated as she was.

He frowned down at her, his at least six foot frame looming over her five foot, one and one quarter inch one. He didn't make the move to go, however, just continued to stare at her. His expression was had to read, though she was certain she could see a hint of interest deep in those smoldering brown eyes. Did she just think, *smoldering*? She licked her lips and watched him follow the action intently, something brighter flashing in his eyes. Oh, yeah, he was interested. She arched her back with the realization of the current resonating between them, a definite live wire, letting a small smile upturn her mouth. Thank goodness she had dressed up a bit tonight in her effort to blend in with the other patrons. She flipped her ponytail over her shoulder in a well-practiced flirty gesture. Always worked.

"What, without your food?" she questioned in mock horror, ready to invite him back to the table. Wouldn't Celine be surprised? The guy was new in town, wasn't it was just being a good neighbor to be friendly?

"I'll stop somewhere else. I'm in kind of a rush. Maybe another time. Do you come here often?"

A harried waitress came bustling up at that moment, mop in hand, ready to deal with the spill. Gabby frowned at the interruption, which forced them to move apart. Just when the evening had gotten a whole lot more interesting.

"Yeah, a couple times a week."

"Then maybe I can hope to see you again."

"Sure." She flashed him a smile that he returned slowly, as if it were an almost forgotten gesture. And this time the smile made it all the way to his eyes, warming them and making the breath still in her body. *Oh, my.*

He left, striding away with all the confidence of a big man who knew how to handle himself. *Very nice.*

"Get what you needed?" Celine asked as Gabby sat at the table, sipping her dirty martini.

"What?" It took her a second. "Ahh. No, no. I didn't."

"What happened? You're the original Quick Draw McGraw on getting the job done."

"Some guy thought I was taking an accidental tumble and he just had to rescue me."

"Nice. What guy?" Celine asked, rubbernecking the crowd.

"He's gone. You know, the guy that was sitting right there." She nodded at the table opposite.

"Really?" Celine's eyebrows rose with her interest. "That hunk. Lucky you!"

"Not so lucky. I lost my chance at an easy photo. Now, I've got to do it again using Plan B."

"Gimme," Celine ordered, wagging her hand at her. "I'll do it. Remember that case you brought me in on last year? You know, before the current state of things."

She appreciated that her sister tiptoed around the sensitive subject, or at least she did most of the time. Sometimes she got on a rant about the absent ex, the direct cause of the current rush of less than desirable cases and more than half the reason she was closed for any new business with a man.

Celine continued her stroll down Memory Lane, her expression smug. "That supposedly bankrupt white-collar defendant who tried to pull the wool over the court's eyes about being unable to afford the fine, and how I helped by posing with you as a potential buyer of a multi-million dollar listing that he forgot to tell the court he was sole owner of? And you know the best part?"

"No, what's the best part?"

"Driving around and playing *Folsom Prison Blues* by Johnny Cash all that week, making it our anthem. We make a good team, sis."

She handed the phone over without comment, her grin wide with the memory. Con man had had it coming, too, his own admission sealing his fate. She'd had a few such satisfying cases and wanted more of that kind of action, taking down criminals who thought themselves above the law.

The line-dancing crew was in Celine's way as she hurried off, wiggling her way through the crowd. Well, they were in everyone's way, strutting to a new tune. *It Wasn't God Who Made Honky Tonk Angels. Oh, really?* Nevertheless, her toe-tapping began again in earnest. A sudden wild urge came over Gabby to join them and, before she knew it, she was dancing with the crowd, using the rhythmic, fun movements to absorb the excess energy surging through her system. Sometimes it was great to be alive.

Her sister came back just as the tune ended. She plonked onto her chair, breathing hard. "Look-y here!" She handed over Gabby's phone.

Gabby checked it out. The photo showed Mr. Smith in full working mode, making an octopus look handicapped by comparison. "It'll work."

"A little thank you wouldn't hurt." Celine flounced in her seat, giving her that look. The one that annoyed Gabby. Like Celine was the put-upon step-sister in a fairy tale.

"Thank you, Celine. You are *so* good at this I have no idea why you don't give up your day job working in that dead-end place as a PI's office assistant when you know darn well you've got the skills to do so much more and come work for me full-time. Oh, yeah, right, you like to eat too much." As soon as the words had left her mouth, she wanted to recall them.

"Sorry." Gabby rubbed the back of her neck, a pair of eyes and the whiff of real man still front and center in her mind, try as she might to toss them aside. "Business could be better. But I have no right to take it out on you."

Her sister pouted. "Only if you buy me another martini."

She bit her tongue, wincing at the sudden pain. "Okay. One more, but that's it."

She gestured at their waitress, ordering the round with a wiggle of her forefinger, her ringing cell phone demanding her attention. Why hadn't she thought to give the guy her number? Or at least ask his name? But soon as she checked the incoming number, she snatched the phone from the table, forgetting her questions for the moment. Silk O'Connor never called this late.

"Hey, Gabby. Sorry to bother you, but something important has come up."

"You sound rushed. What's going on?" Gabby could hear the new baby crying in the background. Lucky Silk, finding the man of her dreams. The one who wanted the white picket fence with all the trimmings. She sighed. Not her destiny.

"The baby's fussy and we're having company. But that's not why I called you. TETRAD has an important job that's just come up. Tonight. I don't want to discuss the details over the phone. Are you interested? Can we count on you short-term? I've got my hands full with the baby, but I'll help where I can."

"How temporary?" Gabby interrupted.

"Well, it might just lead to a future full-time job with us, Gabby. I know you've been wanting to do more, leave the cheating husbands far behind. We both know you're better than that. Step up now and we'll see how it goes. What do you say? We need you bright and early at the office. Can you manage your current caseload along with an extra assignment that will take up a lot of your time?"

"Yes." Gabby's heartrate sped up. "I say yes. I'll see you in the morning. Oh, and text me the address, please."

She set her phone back on the bar table, giving Celine a wide smile.

"So, what is it? You look like a cat that swallowed the canary, sis."

"Just got a short-term job to work with a new group calling themselves TETRAD. Something that might lead to more if all it goes well. Fingers crossed."

"When do this need you?" Celine asked, leaning forward in her seat, taking a sip of her drink.

"Right away. And they just take big cases, too."

Celine wrinkled her forehead. "TETRAD. Hmm, isn't that the new business your friend Silk is involved with?"

"Yeah. And the best part, what they stand for, their mission of doing whatever it takes to help others, is right up my alley."

The waitress delivered the drinks as if right on cue. Celine raised her glass to toast with her sister.

"To new beginnings," she said, her big blue eyes brimming with enthusiasm, the gold speckles dancing brightly as they caught the reflected light of the rustic chandeliers placed strategically over the tables.

"Yes, to new beginnings." The atmosphere in the bar took on a brighter hue as she let the news infiltrate her system. What could a few more drinks hurt? The crowd was just getting into full swing and another round of dancing would be good exercise. On impulse, she pulled her sister to the dance floor as the house band struck up a new tune, something about a good-hearted woman in love with a two-timing man. Figured, but at least she could dance her ass off, allowing herself the luxury of releasing a little steam for a change. It had been so long since she'd felt the urges she'd been having tonight, overcome with the pure unbridled joy of being young, a life full of potential, excitement, and purpose lie dead ahead.

* * * *

Day Three: 1:22 a.m.

A bit tipsy and having caught a taxi home, Gabby stumbled into the bedroom of her rented townhouse. She pulled off her boots and tossed them aside. Her dress vanished next and she lay down on the bed in just her white lace panties and bra. What a fun night. Worth being a little tired in the morning. Too bad that handsome stranger on his big white horse had had to leave so soon. Gabby giggled aloud at the idea of the man on a horse galloping through the Legend Saloon.

Celine was wrong about her. Gabby knew lust—she was just picky. Very picky. What was wrong with that? Her fingers drifted to her lips. The stranger had stared at them, his eyes all dark and smoldering as though he'd been imagining kissing her. Oh, he'd been thunderstruck too, no doubt. *Damn, I wish he was here right now.* He looked experienced, as if he knew his way around a woman's body. *Would know just what buttons to push, what areas to concentrate on most. Oh, yeah.*

Her hands drifted farther down and she grasped her full breasts, imagining his big strong hands there in place of hers. *Caressing, touching, kissing me all over.* She let her hands do what she wanted his to. Tugging on her erect nipples, first with his oh-so-talented fingers, then with his firm, sweet lips. He would pull down the straps of her bra, exposing her naked breasts. He'd suck gentle at first, then more fiercely, ever so exquisitely hard on her sensitive nipples until she begged him for mercy. For him to fuck her. Fuck her hard, and fuck her long. *Oh, yeah.*

His spectacular package came to mind, how large it looked. She wanted what was hidden behind that zipper to come out and play. Now. To push between her legs, thrust right into and stretch her pussy lips wide open. Gabby inched her hand farther down her body and under the top edge of her panties. Then down inside the thin cloth, searching for the swollen lips, finding herself ready. She used her fingers to spread her outer lips, slipping one finger inside her pussy while the other caressed her clit.

She stroked her nub, her fingers rubbing it in small, tight circles, eliciting a low moan from her throat as she arched off the bed. *Oh, so good.* Gabby imagined him using his tongue to nibble at the sensitive bundle of nerve endings. Pleasure streaked through her as she envisioned his lips tugging, causing even more throbbing, more moans to escape. She moved her hand quicker, two fingers plowing into her heat, legs spread wide. She was soaking wet, her pussy lips slick and hot, her body about to explode.

Yes. Yes. Yes. Fuck me harder. And he did, his cock so massive it filled her to the brim, rubbing against her G-spot until she was a seething, undulating woman on fire with lust. No self-control left, no sense of false modesty — she let him do what he wanted. *Anything. Everything. Just do me.* Then he pinched her clit with the perfect amount of pressure, sending her reeling into a mind-blowing orgasm that shook her to the core, leaving her breathless. *Wow.* She fell back against the cover. She now had her new bedtime fuck buddy.

Despite that, she still spent a restless night, stuck in the same loop of gal meets guy and instead of avoiding the lust, beds him and finds him amazing in the sack. It was so good, in fact, that she needed a cold shower in the morning to get a grip and remind herself no man could be that good at going downtown. Gabby grumbled at Celine for the stupid suggestion.

She pulled into the parking lot of the address Silk had texted. *Nice.* The group had set up shop in a commercial strip mall on Granville Island a few weeks back. Central location, nondescript with subtle signage — perfect for their operations. She spied Silk's silver Audi and Jake's black SUV. A GMC Sierra 1500 half-ton, unknown to her, was parked in the same line-up. In her overnight text giving the business address, Silk had mentioned they were bringing in a heavy hitter.

Silk stood near the front of the minimalist, ultra-modern store as Gabby opened the door, stepping inside and relishing the air conditioning cooling her agitated skin. Silk was so busy talking to someone she missed her entrance. Gabby moved to the side to check out who it was who had her friend so engaged.

No. Fucking. Way. Can't be him. But it was him. The man who had haunted her dreams all night long. Oh,

God, and she had gotten herself off, imagining him having his way with her.

She swallowed, her skin tingling and her heat rising as her heartrate sky-rocked into the stratosphere. God, if he knew how much he'd figured in her going-downtown reality and very wet dreams last night, he'd be running for his life. At that precise moment, he looked over at her, his eyes widening just a little. *Quick, think of something else. Anything else.*

She frowned. Was the universe setting her up just for fun? If there are no coincidences, what the fuck was this?

"Gabby, good morning." Silk woke up to the fact she was standing there.

"Morning," she mumbled.

"We were just talking about you, how you've agreed to help us this week. I'd like you to meet Cole McClintock. Cole, this is Gabrielle Banks. An awesome private investigator with myriad skills, not to mention a good friend."

Cole cleared his throat, his expression surprised. "Hi."

"Hi, again," Gabby said, wishing she could sink right through the floor and into the basement. Of all the men it could be. The guy that Silk had been raving on about since he'd helped Jake and Silk take down the cartel in LA, telling her how much they wanted him to join with their new consortium. So, this was that guy. The one with intimate knowledge of the law and superior tech skills who'd helped them in LA. The very man she'd most want to make a good first impression on. Too late for that. If she didn't need this job so damn much, she would turn and walk out the door, knowing all too well that people form their first impression of a person in the first ten or eleven seconds of meeting, and, worse, that it was tough to change that impression. *Talk about embarrassing.* God, how she must have appeared last night on the job—dressed like a slut to attract a guy's interest for a honey trap sting.

"You two know each other?" Silk asked, straightening her ponytail. Gabby shifted her focus with difficulty to her friend. She looked good—still losing the baby weight, but happiness shone from every pore. Gabby pushed aside a slight stab of jealousy. Her friend deserved her happiness. Silk had been through so much. Hell, she was all alone in the world, thanks to a drunk driver who'd killed her pregnant sister back in LA. Silk had earned her new contentment by choosing the right guy, though the way she told it, she'd had no choice. They'd combusted on the world's strangest first meeting, bar none.

Silk had 'fessed up to Gabby about her insanity at the courthouse where she planned to take out the man responsible for killing her sister. How she'd waited with a high-powered rifle a block away. That sounded unbelievable to Gabby, knowing her friend and her normal demeanor. Then, three days undercover immersed in each other's company, and they'd been an item ever since. A definite fairy-tale ending. One in a gazillion.

"Kind of. We met last night at the Legend Saloon, just not formally. We had a slight accident with a food order," Gabby explained.

She snuck a look at Cole. He was frowning, not a good sign, his arms crossed in front of his chest. What was he thinking? Nothing good, she'd hazard a bet. *Of all the times to meet a possible future boss.* She'd better sort this out as best she could. If only she didn't need this opportunity so much. She hated being judged more than anything. Her ire rose at the idea. What right did he have to criticize her? He didn't know her circumstances. How she slaved for every penny to pay off a mountain of debt.

"Yeah, I was on one of those stakeouts, you know, dressed to catch a cheating husband. What can I say? They pay the bills." She shrugged, clicking a thumb nail against her front teeth and sneaking another glance at Cole, who was still frowning, but looking less judgmental. *Easy for you, Texas. You don't have to pay for an ex.*

Silk laughed, giving Cole a slight shake of her head as if it was no big deal, a definite signal. "What? That was you? We ended up with McDonald's. Not exactly my favorite to-die-for pulled pork sandwich, but it sure beat cooking last night. Cole Quintin Jake Marshall, named after my three favorite guys in the whole world, was not in the best of moods. I hope you finished with the case, caught the guy? I know you're not big on spending nights in the bar. Hazard of the job, eh."

At least Texas wasn't frowning now, though he still looked skeptical. Well, it was a start. Maybe. Resentment scorched the earth she stood on. *Fuck. Fuck. Fuck.*

"Sorry about that. I'll make it up to you, I promise." So, this was also one of the guys they'd named their son after. The realization sent another shockwave reverberating through her system. It just got better and better.

"No worries. Okay, let's head into the conference room and we'll lay the case out for you," Silk said.

Gabby hurried after her friend when Cole gestured for her to precede him, then following close behind them into the impressive room that housed a large oval teak table with sleek chrome and black leather chairs. She caught a whiff of his fragrance, relishing the fresh scent of clean man so early in the morning. *Hmm.* Conflicting signals entered her brain, one demanding she push him down on the conference table and have her way with him and the other wanting her to try to appear more ladylike and make up for last night. It made her head spin.

Silk O'Connor's husband, Jake Marshall, appeared, opening the back door to the office from the warehouse side, his boots echoing on the hardwood floor, cell phone in his hand. He gave his wife a quick peck on the cheek, nodded a quick greeting at Gabby. *Ah, Jake.* He was one of the few remaining good guys, the guy who wore a big white hat for her friend Silk. Was that what she wanted as well? If she were a betting woman, she'd lay a billion to one odds against it happening for her. *Ever.*

"Okay, here's the deal."

"Jake, can I speak with you for a moment — outside?" Cole asked, interrupting him.

Jake looked surprised but gave a curt nod. Both men strode out of the room, carefully closing the door behind them. *Fuck, I know what that's about.*

Gabby gave Silk a skeptical glance, biting at her thumb nail in earnest now. "I don't think that guy's too pleased about my being here."

"No worries. He just doesn't know you yet. Give him a chance. He'll come around once he realizes how skilled and talented you are. How could he not? Look at you!"

"Maybe." Fuming at the perceived slight, wondering at what was being said, Gabby drummed her fingers on the tabletop.

"Relax. It's going to be fine."

Oh, yeah, I can see that.

The two men came back into the room a few minutes later, sitting down as if nothing untoward had happened. Her stomach roiled, making her want to strike out at something. Anything. *Just – stay – calm.* So much easier said than done. She shook her head, focusing only on Jake, desperate to avoid looking at the guy who doubted her. *I might not be a good judge of men, but damn it, I'm good at my job.*

"Quinn's in the field and can't join us just yet." She knew Quinn, the ex-FBI guy who'd also been on the sting in LA with the pair. Jake continued, "Okay, Gabby, let's bring you up to speed on what Cole's shared with us. We got something huge that Cole's brought to our attention that needs to be done yesterday. Missing fifteen-year-old child, tied to tech blackmail. We brought you in today not just because we're underpowered with Silk working only part-time but because we have real need of your skill set—our specialized knowledge in surveillance and undercover operations plus your ability to read people. Knowing the tells, if they're lying or not during conversations and interviews."

Gabby nodded and caught Cole staring at her, an unfathomable expression in his eyes. He broke the connection first and she allowed herself a small victory smile. *Don't look too shabby now, eh, Texas?*

Jake continued, looking at Cole now, "Were you able to contact the ghost?"

"*Ghost?*" she repeated. What the hell were they talking about?

"Satoshi Nakamoto." Cole gave her a sidelong glance. "The man behind the bitcoin gold rush who's the only one alive who can do what the blackmailers want. And that's break into the original source code and plant a bug to drain off funds without it being discovered. No,

I've left a message. He usually gets back to me within twelve hours. We'll hear soon."

"Good," Jake grunted. "Okay, Gabby. I want to see how it goes, you working with us, you know, during the next while. I think this case will be a test for all of us and if you become a vital part of your team, pull your own weight—" He gave Cole a glance. "Then we'll look at turning this into a full-time job. Does that work for you? Gives you a chance to see if you like working with us, as well. Sound fair?"

"Yeah, sure, I get it. It works for me." She got it all right. Cole was the perpetrator genius behind the probation period. Well, she'd show him! She was the real deal.

"I want you and Cole working together, staking out Chinatown. This has come down so quickly we haven't even had time to outfit surveillance vans, so, Cole, you'll need to use the truck this week, and a huge thank you from us that you took the time to install some vital equipment last night. Plus, we need to hire office staff like yesterday." *No. Not him. I can work by myself, thank you very much.* She kept her objections from showing with great difficulty, biting down hard on the inside of her mouth, the metallic taste that flooded her mouth souring her mood further.

"How was she taken?" Gabby asked, wincing from the instant pain. She needed to get all the facts. Fast. Even the smallest detail could matter in solving a case. She pulled out her iPhone to take notes.

"Outside a school dance. Prom night, in fact. Made it too easy, knowing the place and time. Why don't you fill Gabby in with all the details, Cole? It will save valuable time and Quinn won't be back until later. I'm on my way out to make some arrangements. Oh, and

I'd better send you a photo of Sara." He stared at his phone, working the keys.

"Sure," Cole agreed, his tight expression not giving anything away as he waited for Jake to finish the task.

Things were happening at a dizzying speed. But with a young girl missing, there was no time for any hesitation. On her part, either. She needed to get over herself, be the professional she knew herself to be. "Okay, whatever you need, Jake, I'll do my best."

Jake nodded with satisfaction as he finished with his phone, sealing the deal by shaking Gabby's hand. "Okay, good, welcome aboard. I'm confident you'll want to join us permanently after a few days working together." He leaned over and kissed Silk again. "Catch you later, baby doll." He was gone in a flash out of the front door.

"And I have to check on the baby. You okay if I leave, Gabby? Cole can get you up to speed. I'll be back in an hour or so. I just need to go nurse my son."

The hairs on the back of Gabby's neck tingled. *Alone with dream guy. Oh, great.* Yes, she'd have to get over herself — him, too, when a young girl needed their help.

"Okay. Fill me in on all you know," she said, turning around and facing the enemy square on.

"Have you read *The Art of War*, Gabrielle?"

"No, why? And it's just Gabby."

"One of the questions that is asked by Sun Tzu, the Chinese general who wrote the classic work during the Chou Dynasty around 500 BC is, which side are the officers and men more highly trained?"

"Okay, you've hooked me. Explain."

"Jake's filled me in, telling me about what you've accomplished at such a young age. Quite remarkable."

"What?" She didn't like that, not one little bit. It made the earth feel less stable beneath her feet. Even though she spent her days researching others, she hated the tables turned on her, having others discuss her. She might have suspected what was being said behind the closed door a few minutes ago, but it was a different thing to have it confirmed. "Why would you need to question my abilities?" Hands on hips, she glared at him across the short distance that separated them. "Don't you trust Jake to hire good people."

"I needed your measure. And I was pleasantly surprised to discover just how accomplished you are. With you being a friend of Silk, I was worried nepotism was involved."

"What the fuck? Thanks a lot. What about you? Aren't you a friend, as well? Didn't they even name their baby after you?"

"Excuse me. I'm complimenting you here. Your work in the private investigator field has been outstanding. Well, most of the time, anyway. Lately you've been working some cases that are questionable at best."

"They pay the bills." She hated having to defend working high-profile divorce cases. But the ex had tarnished her reputation, making her persona non-grata in some circles. She'd had to go it on her own without the benefit of partners, until now. And she was not going to let his doubts spoil her chances. *No fucking way.*

He went on as if she hadn't interjected. "Your work solving that wrongful death case and discovering the offender was still alive, saving the insurance company millions, was outstanding. And the guy had gone to a lot of trouble, setting up a fake mugging death in a foreign country. Even finding out he'd bought a body and involved the coroner shows remarkable skill. Bribed officials don't like to be challenged. Then to discover the connection to the upper echelons of government. Damn fine work."

"You know about that? Yeah, well, I have my moments. And I really hate fraud of any kind. He was also blackmailing his wife's family into being accomplices, threatening a small child. Fucking monster, in my opinion. Got what he deserved and I hope he rots in jail. What else have you got but your honor and reputation in the end? And your family, of course."

Cole turned pale. In an instant. A darkness slithered across behind his eyes before he turned away. What was the deal with him? She needed to ask Silk what she knew about him as soon as Sara was back home.

He cleared his throat, his eyes hardening. "Okay, let's discuss the particulars of this case. Ready? Let's head into the back so you can see the rest of the operation."

"I was born ready." It didn't come out quite right, but she just followed him through the back door of the storefront and into the warehouse behind.

A huge bank of computers and other high-tech equipment filled a good portion of the space. The air buzzed with expectations of something huge being accomplished.

She turned to Cole after plunking herself down in one of the half-dozen aerodynamic chairs. "Okay, fill me in. Start right at the beginning."

He obliged, sitting down opposite her, bracing himself on the armrests. The man was so tense the corded muscles of his impressive forearms were clearly visible below the edge of the sleeve of his black T-shirt. And he was so tall his knees projected outward while she had to sit forward to keep her feet on the ground. She watched for other tells as he spoke. Passionate about saving the fifteen-year-old victim, of course, and dedicated to making sure Sara got home to her family before the deadline. Same as she was.

"Quinn Malone, the former FBI special agent that Jake and Silk worked with in LA?"

She nodded. Silk had filled her in on his involvement months back. It was the main reason they'd asked him to become a partner with them.

"He's fairly certain the problem arose in Chinatown — that one or more of the BTK gang members set up the abduction, right here in Vancouver. He's in the field right now checking into it."

"How does he know this?" She pursed her lips as she asked and earned his quick glance at her mouth. *Hmm. Interesting. Not as cool a cucumber as he lets on.*

"Some intel he's been party to. He learned about them while working for the FBI in their gang investigation unit. Apparently, the gang's widespread in the US. Began its reign of terror in New York City. And it's spread to Toronto here, as well. Quinn's knowledge is invaluable."

It was all business now as Gabby racked her brain for every bit of intel she knew about their illicit activities. "Hmm, BTK…mostly money laundering, drugs and prostitution, some real estate deals, all run here in Canada by Wu Chang and his clan for the past two decades They own Five Star Tower on the waterfront, and some buildings in the downtown core, chiefly the Red Dragon in the garment district, according to my source at the *Vancouver Herald*. Leanne Reimer, a columnist at the newspaper. She and I go way back. We both have an interest in seeing justice done, and this guy has been on our radar for some time."

Cole nodded, an eyebrow raised.

"Also, their MO includes demanding protection money from businesses from people who don't trust law enforcement to have their best interests. Chinatown is so insular that it causes all sorts of trouble for the regular people, good people, people just wanting to come to this country and make a decent living for their families. And don't get me started on the exploitation of young women by men like Chang, demanding they work exclusively for his operations in payment for passage. But, same old shit that's been going down for what seems like forever in most cities on the planet. It all needs to stop—be exposed to the light of day."

She paused, considering, hand on her chin. "But there's more to this than just the BTK gang. I'd bet they just provided the muscle because it's not their usual MO asking for bitcoins. I'm guessing this will lead all the way back to mainland China. Perhaps the triad?"

"Yeah, I'd say that's an accurate guess. Some big player wants an easy way to siphon off funds to an off-shore account. Smart thinking—long-term." Cole rubbed at his jaw, giving her a speculative glance. *Clean-shaven this morning.* She'd been wrong about him doing a fancy razor job. He'd just not shaved for a couple of days when she'd seen him last night. She preferred a clean-shaven face anyway. Less razor burn. She swallowed, last night's dream loop still too fresh in her mind. She forced it away. *Keep a lid on it, Gabby.*

"Yeah, but maybe not smart short-term, since we're all going to be hot on his thieving ass!" She couldn't help giving Cole a wicked grin. His eyes widened just a tad. It was the first moment of levity between them and she relished the way one corner of his mouth twitched upward. Good. Whatever he'd lived through—and she could tell by the dark shadows lurking in his eyes that it had been bad—fucking bad— he was still capable of seeing humor. She vowed right then to work on that. See if she could make him at least give one good belly laugh after they'd brought Sara home.

Cole came closer, reaching around her for something lying on the desk behind her. It took her off-guard as he was all of a sudden in her personal space. His tantalizing fragrance filled her nostrils, making them flare. She was certain she caught his nose twitching, as well.

He held up some tiny electronics she knew had been designed for gathering information from a fair distance for her inspection. "We're going to be planting some of these Acute 5000 babies today. Get some intel."

She nodded, not trusting herself to speak, her panties wetting from the heat of such close contact. Just great. Now, she'd need to invest in clean underwear. And, if they were going to be spending days locked together in the truck doing intensive surveillance on BTK, she'd better buy lots and lots of pairs. Just what she needed, another expense.

A noise in the outer office announced company and she hopped off her chair to check on the visitor, thankful for the interruption.

Chapter Three

Day Three: 9:38 a.m.

Cole watched her leave, her tiny body sizzling with energy as she strode across the cement floor of the warehouse, still wearing the cowgirl boots of the night. Instead of the enticingly skimpy yellow sundress, she now wore a knee-length denim skirt, and a red silk blouse that hugged her curves. She was unlike any woman he'd met with those fuck-me boots, sexy, wild yet constrained hair that he'd love to see down and feisty attitude. Not to mention those clear blue eyes that reminded him of a summer morning. If she only knew what had transpired last night after meeting her, a hot piece he figured for an empty-headed though intriguing party girl. *Fuck.*

Dreaming of pushing her up against a wall, having her on the floor, in his bed, planting his face in her sweet pussy as she spread herself wide open for him, giving him a view of her slick pink center, her nipples budding under his finger. Having her every which way, filling her with his cock. His balls tingled with the memory, his cock going hard for the umpteenth time since they'd met. Had that just been last night? *Double fuck.*

He had to keep himself in check, even if he had to masturbate three times a day, every day, until this was over. Which might not even be enough, considering what she was doing for his libido. Maybe he should invest in saltpeter? Reduce his carnal urges before they got out of hand and he pounced on her in a moment of weakness, embarrassing everyone in the process. But still, he had to wonder, was she as good in bed as she looked? Because if she was, he was lost. *Oh, Jesus, I could lose myself in a woman like that.*

But, he had to admit as he positioned himself more comfortably, willing his hard-on away with great difficulty, there was something more to her than her obvious beauty and sexiness that now piqued his interest. Her passion, drive, and commitment to catch bad guys, whatever it took, was clear in her intelligent eyes as she spoke. But was she the right woman for a case like this? Even given the facts Jake had shared a few minutes ago? He shook his head with worry. That remained to be seen.

A few seconds later, she came back with Quinn in tow. Quinn's expression tight, he nodded at Cole, who shifted his thoughts to the case, where he vowed they were going to stay. *No time for foolishness.* "Morning, I've just come from Chinatown and a trail that led down to the docks, but it petered out. How's things going with the tech situation? Any word from your guy?" Quinn asked.

"Just waiting to hear back," Cole grunted. "Explain what you found out."

Quinn pursed his lips, shaking his head, his deep brown eyes fierce with intensity. The last time Cole had seen him, he'd sported a short military haircut, faded jeans and black Henley T-shirt accompanied by a tactical multi-pocketed canvas vest and lace-up boots. Today it was the same, minus the vest. By his six foot, three inch muscular frame that rivaled his own, it was obvious he worked out and could handle himself. And Cole knew from personal experience it was the truth. Quinn was a man he'd follow into battle anytime, anywhere.

"The talk on the street is about what you would expect. No one's talking, obviously scared of retaliation from the BTK gang. But I'm damn certain that something's being covered up. A lot of tells in the eyes of the merchants I questioned that they were hiding information. Years of experience handling interrogations for the FBI made that abundantly clear."

He paused for a deep breath. "That damn Born to Kill gang. Started in New York City in the seventies, the target of a massive sting in the early nineties, now it's reared its head again. Though the group that's taken on the moniker is not Vietnamese this time, but mainly Chinese." Quinn might be repeating what they already knew, but still, the stark words rang harsh and expressions sobered further.

"Go on," Cole said.

"I've narrowed the place of operations down to a couple of businesses. Chang's Café and Paradise Massage. Both run by Wu Chang, the man I suspect having something to do with this. He's known as 'Uncle' to the local people in the neighborhood and is feared and respected. He's the head boss, their number-one guy, and the only one with enough muscle to carry off the kidnapping. We'll need to get inside both locations and plant bugs in hopes of picking up some chatter about what's going down. Today. I don't think I have to remind anyone that the clock is ticking."

Cole nodded. "Yes, I can take care of —"

"That's my job. I'm filling in for Silk and that's what she does," Gabby interrupted him.

Cole shook his head. "Absolutely not! Massage parlors are often fronts for prostitution, especially when they're run by a gang as this one appears to be."

"What, you don't think I can handle myself?" she challenged, arching her eyebrows.

"It's not that. It's a seedy, dangerous place for a young woman. Makes more sense if I get inside as a customer. Quicker and cleaner."

She frowned at him, her baby blue eyes narrowing and taking on a dangerous glint. "Silk went right into the lion's den in LA. Got the deed done. I'm more than capable of doing the same. I can handle myself. I've had lots of tactical training, including advanced self-defense and jujitsu."

He wanted to say that Silk had been deep in a revenge psychosis at the time that Jake had rescued her and kept her from an action she would not have been able to take back. But he didn't. Being one of Silk's close friends, Gabby already knew. He'd opened his mouth to offer more objections when Quinn interrupted, flashing him a warning with his eyes.

"Fine. I think Cole should do the massage parlor as the chance of them hiring outside the immigrant population is slim, while you, Gabby, can do the café," Quinn said. "If that doesn't work, we'll figure out something else. But be ready for both points of entry before you leave here with plenty of tech equipment. Cole, have you got access to enough electronics to do the job? We're going to have to go at this full bore.

There's no time to be caught with our pants down, unprepared."

"Sure, I have everything even remotely necessary." The café couldn't be as dangerous as the massage parlor, right? He'd supplied Silk's maid uniform in LA. When she'd come on-board to help, he'd been ready with the goods, having known that was an ideal route in. And it had worked out just fine, though it wasn't the planted bugs that had given over the goods but her tapping into the main circuitry. A vision of Gabrielle in a skimpy uniform giving him a massage slipped into his mind. His groin tightened. *Fuck.* He didn't need that kind of distraction right now. Not with all those images from last night still threatening to send him into overdrive. He absently licked his lips, wanting a taste of her in the worst way.

"Okay, I'll plan to go to the Chang Café and be a customer, dress sexy. Guys in these places only see the body, not the face, anyway." She snorted her disgust. "Then I can plant bugs under a table and in the ladies' bathroom. Or better yet, if they need any waitressing help, I'll jump right in. That way, I can get into the back office. Filling out a job application is an ideal way." Gabby nodded as she detailed her plans.

"If not, we'll go in when the business closes tonight — if it closes. Plan B, but I would prefer not to use it unless necessary as it involves more risk. It's going to be a long day, folks. I wouldn't expect much sleep until we find Sara. Okay, anything else?" Quinn asked.

No one spoke.

"Okay, let's roll."

Cole went right to work collecting the necessary items off the well-stocked shelves he himself had filled scant hours earlier.

His cell phone buzzed and he answered it, tucking it between his chin and his neck to keep his hands free to continue collecting what was needed.

"Hey, Cole," Beau said, loud and clear over the device. He was stunned to hear from his brother today of all days. Or maybe he shouldn't be. Beau never gave a moment's thought to anyone but himself.

"Beau? Why are you calling?" Cole asked, keeping his tone flat. It was not what he wanted to know most. When he'd been going through the worst trials of his life, his twin had been nowhere to be seen. His identical twin brother—a mirror image only on the outside. Inside, they couldn't have been more different.

"I'm thinking of coming to Vancouver to see you. What do you say?"

Cole closed his eyes, gritting his teeth. Where the hell was Beau when he needed him most? Oh, yeah, right, back in rehab for the third time. "A little busy right now. There's a young girl missing and I'm on the job. The clock's ticking. Might be better if you held off on that."

"Oh," Beau said, clearing his throat. "I really wanted to see you, to try to make amends, Cole. To try to make up for not being there when Maddie died. I was in rehab and my counselor said it was too early to risk it. I wanted to come, I really did—"

"No matter. What's done is done. I have to go. Catch you later." Cole broke off the call and slid the cell into his jeans pocket.

He looked up to catch Gabrielle staring at him, her lips pressed together, though she didn't remark on the terse conversation.

"I need to stop by my place on the way, to change. In case I need to apply for a job."

"Fine, but it's a waste of time. I could easily do both places."

"I carry my own weight. The café will be perfectly safe this time of day, anyway. We've both got jobs to do, so let's get to it."

Cole nodded. "Okay. Here you go, Gabrielle," he said, handing her a supply of electronics while pocketing his own.

"It's Gabby," she said, arching her eyebrows. "I think I mentioned that already."

"Doesn't seem to fit you."

She grinned at him. "I can talk with the best of them."

"Fine. If you insist, Gabby it is."

She chewed on her bottom lip, drawing his attention once more to how full and soft they looked. He liked that she wore no lipstick. He hated sticking to lip gloss. *Now, where the fuck did that idea come from? Mind on job.*

"Okay, let's go," he said more grumpily than intended.

"Sure," she said, looking more confused than anything. He was so out of practice with women. Well, it was staying that way. Best she think him an asshole than anything else. He'd lost his white hat a long time ago. It had been ground down into the dust.

He followed her out onto the street, locking the door behind them. With Silk still a no-show, the office was deserted until they hired more help. He used his key fob to unlock his half-ton and moved to help Gabby inside, but she was too fast for him. Climbing up and perching on the passenger side seat with ease, she'd soon buckled herself in and was waiting for him to come around and start up the engine.

The drive was made in silence, and twenty minutes later, the heavens opened and rain sluiced down as Cole pulled into a parking spot in front of Gabby's townhouse. No wonder their official tourism website listed ten things to do on a rainy day in Vancouver. They needed to. The east coast location was notorious for rainfall, something he'd have to get used to after dry Los Angeles and its Santa Ana winds. Of course, rain might beat a raging wildfire all to hell. Or an earthquake.

"Do you want to come up while I change?" she asked, giving him a sidelong glance.

"Ah, no, I'd better wait here. And you'd better put on a rain slicker." He awarded himself several brownie points for resisting the urge to say yes.

"Sure, boss," she said, her white teeth flashing and giving him other ideas. He watched her disembark, race up the front steps and gain access to the front door, the drenching downfall plastering the silk blouse to her body in mere seconds, making his eyes widen. He swallowed hard. She vanished inside and he drummed his fingers on the steering wheel, waiting, wishing he had accepted her invite. Might be nice to check out her apartment, see how she lived.

She didn't keep him waiting long, hurrying back down the front steps in a yellow rain jacket pulled tight over her body. She jumped back in the front cab of the truck and shrugged off the bright coat. He took in her clothing choice and damn near forgot to breathe.

* * * *

Day Three: 10:59 a.m.

"'Study the past if you would define the future'. Know who say that?" Uncle Chang asked the three young men crowded round the tiny table in the back of Chang's Café.

Tommy shrugged with politeness when Uncle looked his way. Uncle began most meetings with some – in his opinion – unnecessary quote, his dark eyes glittering as he dispelled his wisdom.

When no one answered his query, Uncle shook his head in sadness. "We are doomed to repeat our mistakes if we don't study our history. Confucius say it and many other wise things. Very smart man with admirable character. Better than fine manners that pass for good man here. Five thousand years of history. Sima Qian, he wrote the records down way back in the day." He tapped the side of his head. "We know more than others. Lots more. We skeptical of everything. Choose what's right."

"Wikipedia says that time is not right. Says it's only thirty-five hundred years. Why, Uncle?" Lee asked in all innocence, not understanding things yet in Canada and daring his uncle's wrath. Lee was newer to the BTK than Tommy. Uncle had already explained to him that the country was a baby with no real sense of history. Not like the Chinese who know so much and had so much culture. Going way back. The idea gave him a proper footing, made him a stronger person, for sure.

"Fuck that stupid thing! Don't know nothing about us. Written by people with no past. Stay away from it or you get yourself stupid. Understood?"

Lee looked down at the tabletop, chastised, his Adam's apple bobbing up and down as he swallowed. A sheen of sweat broke out on his forehead beneath his black spiky hair. He had much to learn. Way more than him.

Uncle wasn't done yet. "We Hans are the true people. Look at our art, our writings, our food – we the best. Everyone knows this. We Middle Kingdom. Center of the universe."

A moment of silence.

"Bah, people know nothing of how hard it was growing up in Guangdong province during the civil war. My own grandfather died of pneumonia, leaving our family to fend for ourselves. The things my family had to do to survive, to have a chance at sending one son to land of golden opportunity to help others." Chang shook his head. "We never speak of outside our clan. And the good fortune of Uncle Woo bringing my father here to Vancouver, only fifteen years old with eight dollars in pocket — that was our salvation. My father worked eighteen-hour day to make enough to keep family alive in China. And now, we all here. I sponsor more family. Earn the money to provide. As all of you must do to support our clan."

"What can we do for you today, Uncle? We're here to help in any way," the man Tommy knew as Fat Boy asked, nodding with respect. Fat Boy had been around longer than him, being two years older. Tommy watched the man, who was neither fat nor a boy, wanting to be certain of Fat Boy's lesser importance to BTK, see if he could keep it from growing any stronger.

He patted himself on the back that he was Chang's real nephew. He'd heard the family story countless times in a far more intimate setting, as Uncle loved to lay out a feast for his clan every month without fail. Loved to be the big man. *Big man stuck in the past.* Like this story, told over and over, something Tommy had to hide his distaste for. He prided himself on his smart plan, a plan that was going along with such perfection he felt emboldened at his ability to carry it out. He was destined for greater things, just like the man said. Soon, very soon, he would be ready to step into the open with his cunning revealed, gain the good wishes of the clan, all while filling their coffers with gold.

Chang heaved a heavy sigh. "We must prepare special message, many special message. All of you gather supplies today, go to different stores all over town so no one knows. Make them and stock them in boxes in basement. Right here." He used his forefinger for emphasis, pointing downward. Tommy was aware a vast network of underground rooms and tunnels running beneath Chinatown that kept certain kinds of business for the gang secret. Lots of caverns to hide whatever they needed, even if a war went on for a long time. "If bloody triad think they can come in and push us out, they are much mistaken. We fight. We keep what is ours. Do this right, my boys, and you will get more of the pie."

Tommy sat up straighter. *Special message.* The phrase ping-ponged back and forth in his brain. *Code for delivering a homemade bomb.* A deadly contraption created in a large glass jar that held a stick of dynamite upright with a five-inch fuse surrounded by hundreds of small nails or tacks, then wrapped in duct tape. Something he had not been called upon to do before. Meaning something big was up. So, the threat of triad taking over what was theirs had become real? For months now, there had been rumors. Uncle was too stuck in the past. Old man. Not up on cybercrime. Not like triad. Not like big man in China. Someday Tommy planned on being the big man in Chinatown, and he knew how. Stay up with the times. Keep up with where the money was. Money for far less risk. Nice and clean. Very smart.

His thoughts quickened. *Deliver special message.* Being asked to do such a thing meant he was being trusted more, becoming an important part of the main crew. Good. This would keep Uncle busy, not notice everything else going on. He pushed everything else away and focused on the opportunity of earning a larger piece of the pie if he did this assignment well, helping others to make the rounds to collect protection money from the businesses in the neighborhood. He licked his lips. It also meant more risk, making bombs, but he was the important fire rat.

"I am ready to step up, Uncle," Tommy said, locking eyes with the man and giving a generous head bow.

"Good. You go with him, Fat Boy. Let me know when it is done." Chang grinned. "Fire rat nephew is perfect for this job, eh?"

Chapter Four

Day Three: 11:29 a.m.

"Okay, you wait here. I'll be back as soon as I can." Cole checked his pockets, his hands searching out the bugs he intended to plant wherever possible. He'd parked down the street from Paradise Massage. The rain continued in torrents, so he reached down and grabbed the umbrella that was essential equipment in the rainy city from the side pocket of the driver's door, preparing to exit. Arriving soaking wet would not aid his cause.

"I'm going to grab a coffee and muffin at the café. Want anything?" Gabby asked, pulling on her rain slicker. He couldn't stop himself from turning and watching the performance, her breasts almost falling out of the too-tight top and her creamy thighs visible beneath the scandalously short skirt. A fuck-me outfit if he'd ever seen one. Did she need to go that far to get a job at the café? Now, he was worried she'd make the wrong impression. If she made him hard in an instant, what about every male in a ten-block radius? *Christ.* And he was expected to spend long hours with her. How in the hell was he going to manage that?

"Uh, sure. Coffee black and whatever muffin looks freshest. Doesn't matter. Just be careful, okay?" He got out and shut the truck door harder than necessary before she could answer. He needed to find a boxing gym and wear off some of this tension. He rolled his shoulders and forged on through the downpour, the rain skipping back up from the cement jungle and soaking the bottom of his jeans. The odor of fried food assailed his nostrils, driving away the tantalizing fragrance of Gabby's delicate floral perfume.

Two blocks through the driving rain and he came to the inset doorway with the Paradise Massage sign perched overhead. The business name was arranged around a single red rose motif, and flashed its constant message of twenty-four hour massage available. He pulled the door open, the jingling of bells atop the door planted to alert those inside to customers. The narrowness of the front reception area had a claustrophobic atmosphere, giving Cole a foreboding sense of oppression he had no choice but to ignore. He'd never liked small spaces to begin with and knowing what likely went on behind these dingy walls did nothing for his comfort. A small middle-aged woman wearing a red dress with a white embroidered flower motif greeted him from behind a counter. She gave him a small bob of her head, her black hair pulled up into a sleek bun. On top of the counter was a cash register and some white and green mints in a candy dish. Behind the woman was a display of prices written on four-by-eight chalk board. It looked like the prices changed quite a lot — that area was much smudged next to the written services of time and activities ranging from massage to acupuncture.

"Special price for new customer today only. Only one hundred dollars for a whole hour of massage, includes making sure you are relaxed with full satisfaction guaranteed. Your choice of girl. You like?" the woman asked with politeness, her dark eyes glittering in the dim light of the storefront.

He nodded, placing the closed umbrella he'd been careful to secure before he'd walked into the business, dropping it into the stand provided. He didn't need the bad karma of an open umbrella on his head.

She rang up the cost on the till, waiting while he dug out his wallet. He paid in two fifty-dollar bills, making her smile.

"Come, you choose your girl," she said, gesturing for him to follow her down the hallway. Unnoticed, he stuck a listening bug under the edge of the front counter, then hurried after the woman.

She ducked inside an entrance way and he stopped next to her, observing the half-dozen young women sitting around the room. As they noticed his arrival, most of the women who had to be cold with their lack of proper clothing, sat up straighter on the sofas or chairs they perched upon, giving him coy smiles. One of the women looked bored by his arrival, averting her eyes to avoid contact.

"Generous man has paid for full service. Treat new customer well," she announced to the room at large, lacing her words with an undercurrent of warning.

Cole pointed at the one most reluctant to do the job. "She'll do."

He earned a quick frown that disappeared in a split second as she pressed her lips together, nodding as if in pain. Disgruntled employees could be the best sources of intel. Either that, or she was not into giving him the full experience today, which was fine. Not that he didn't need it. Just not here.

"Come," she said, standing up on her teetering heels and taking his hand, pulling him into the hallway and right into one of the small cubicles. She motioned him inside, closing the door.

"You take off clothes and put on robe, yes?" she asked, pointing at a small partition with a robe thrown over the top. "I prepare now."

"I'm just looking for a massage—nothing more," he said.

Her eyes widened and she pouted. "No tip in just massage. I can do much more for you. Make sure all your stress gone," she suggested, her eyebrows rising with fake coyness.

"I will tip you if the massage is good. All I need."

"Okay, you change, then."

He walked behind the screen and removed his shirt and shoes, keeping an eye out for the best place to leave a bug. He planted one on the window, attaching it to one of the bars that kept out trouble. But more than here, he needed to get into the back office he'd gotten a glimpse of at the end of the hallway. That was where all the action would take place.

He lay on the massage table, front down, rolling his head to the side to observe the masseuse laying out some oil that smelled of coconut when she popped the lid, and placing a towel nearby.

"There's fifty bucks in it for you, darlin', if you let me sleep for a while after."

She smiled. This time it was genuine. "No worries, you sleep like a baby when I finish."

She began with careful attention, working her slender fingers across the skin of his back and down his upper arms.

"Don't be afraid to work the muscles hard. It's been a tough few months." He might as well get something for the deal.

She massaged his shoulders and back in earnest now, applying pressure just this side of pain. *Perfect.* Except he was too tense to really let go.

"You like your job here?" he asked.

She shrugged. "Job okay."

"You live in Vancouver long?"

"Not long, a few months."

"You like working for Uncle Chang? Does he pay good?"

"Uncle Chang? You know Uncle?" she asked, her tone one of slight surprise.

He shook his head. "Not really. But I heard he owned this place and the Chang Café down the street. That he's an important man in Chinatown."

"Yes, better man to know than triad." She dry-spat on the floor for emphasis. "You turn over now. I do your front?"

"I only need my back done, thanks."

"Why you ask about Uncle?" Her tone had changed and was now edged with a tinge of suspicion.

"I thought you might know him and I was just making conversation to pass the time. Not important. When in Rome, you know." He prayed the man was a frequent visitor. That damn clock, tick-tock tock-tock, added a heavy weight in his mind.

She stayed silent, working hard, earning a good tip. Then she stopped, giving him a final tap on the ass he ignored.

He pretended to drift off, his breathing shallow. She moved around, putting things in order. Just when he thought she'd never leave, she slipped out of the room. He waited a few minutes just in case, then got up, put on his shirt and shoes and left the promised tip. He opened the door and peered into the hallway. No one in sight.

He hurried on tiptoe toward the open office door. In and out, then back to the room, if luck held. Once in the office, he moved out of sight of the doorway and looked around. Its windows were also covered in bars, shutting in the ten-by-twelve space. No back door — not good — but above the desk, he spied an opening with a piece of tiling, filling the two by two-foot square, likely leading to the attic. In one corner rested an ancient safe, in the other a file cabinet. The desk was old and battered, with three folding chairs lined up in front. A sturdy leather chair near the back wall faced the desk and the door.

He planted two bugs in quick order, one in the picture frame across from the leather chair and one behind the desk that was far riskier as he could be spotted from the hall. He moved back into a corner as the sound of tinkling bells. The front door had opened. Another customer? He sidled up to the edge of the door and peered around the frame cautiously, sweating at the thought of exposure. Three men, black ski masks pulled down to obscure their faces and guns in hand, were busy shoving the hostess into the room where the women were gathered. *Fuck.* Not what? He wasn't armed. Big mistake. He should have at least brought a Taser.

He jumped up on the desk, pushed the tile aside, pulling himself up by his hands and shoulders into the crawl space above. It took a few seconds, and with his feet dangling from the ceiling he kept expecting to be spotted, an uncomfortable sensation that grew worse by the second. The low-ceilinged attic was dimly lit and dank with the distinct musty odor of mold and mildew. He had no time to wait for his eyes to adjust, placing the tile back over the opening as fast as possible. He lay down nearby, not wanting to break the old wooden floorboards by standing in one spot. Falling through and crashing back into the room would spell disaster.

Shouts and a gun shot rang out. He froze. *Damn it. Now, what?* As his eyes adjusted, he could see the attic ran all the way to the front street, ending in an air vent over the spot where the sign that shouted out the business exploits inside was fastened. Its slight neon glow shone through the cracks in the wall, leaving a lattice-work of design on the planked floor. He began to crawl in that direction, hoping to spot another way out.

Near the front, and most likely over the counter with the till, was another square tile opening. Thank God. He stifled a sneeze, making his ears pop and hurt from the intense pressure. Listening, he heard the door open again with the tell-tale sound of bells and rushing feet, then the sound of women's voices could be heard. Now or never. If might be his only chance. He was under no illusions about what his crawling around in their attic could lead to, and it would in no way be an offer for another massage.

He pushed aside the tile, lowering himself to the counter, and came eye-to-eye with his masseuse. Her eyes widened with shook. She was about to say something when he clamped his hand over her mouth, feeling like a real shit for doing it. Nothing worse than frightening a woman.

"I won't hurt you. I just need to get out of here. I had nothing to do with this. You understand?" he asked racking his brain for an idea, trying to sound reasonable. "I will give you money if you stay quiet. Meet me at Tim Horton's in thirty minutes. Okay? I can pay you well. But I can also be your worst enemy. Don't scream or else you'll give me no choice but to hurt you." The threat was shitty but necessary—he had mere moments to make his escape or maybe be shot. He hoped she would believe the worst of him, at least for a few precious seconds. Men in the next room barked orders. They would be back any moment.

She nodded, her eyes wide with fear. Out of time, he let her go and held his breath, praying she'd believed him. She remained silent. Stood still. Watched him leave. The door closed behind him, each step he took one second closer to freedom.

On the street and heading down the sidewalk, he took a deep breath, enjoying the rain, trying to calm down. The weather had let up to a fine mist, dampening and cooling his flushed face. He'd left his rain gear inside, small price to pay. He hurried toward the truck, each step feeling like he had a bullseye target painted on his back. The street was quiet, as though everyone knew to stay inside, and he made it to his vehicle safely. But where was Gabby? He'd expected her to be done at the café by now. What if something had gone wrong? What if the masked men had been an attack on Chang's business interests? His heartrate increased triple-time at the idea, thudding loudly as adrenaline kicked back in.

He looked around with deep concern, wondering which direction to look in first, the worry ratcheting back up into the stratosphere. Why was she not in the truck when he specifically said to wait for him soon as she was done? Getting coffee and a muffin couldn't take this long? Maybe she'd been offered a job that started ASAP—not very likely—or maybe, the thought making his stomach roll, she was in real trouble?

* * * *

Day Three: 1:19 p.m.

Gabby sipped her coffee as she strolled down the street. The rain had almost stopped, making the rain jacket almost unnecessary, but she couldn't remove it, considering her clothing choices underneath. Well, not unless she wanted to be suspected of being a hooker. But it had worked, and very well indeed.

She spied Cole near the truck on the sidewalk and broke out into a smile. She'd been productive and rather nosy in a few businesses the past hour and had some significant intel to share he might appreciate. His scowl in return made some of the satisfaction drain away. What was his problem?

"Where the hell have you been?" he asked, his eyes accusing her.

"What's the matter? I've just been walking around, getting a feel for this place, getting inside Chang's office. You know, doing my job," she hissed. Like his job was that hard. She could see how much he appreciated scantily dressed women. She'd seen the once-over he'd given her last night. And wasn't he just hanging around such women? An unwelcome visit

77

from the green-eyed monster brought her up short, bit her in the ass. She pressed her lips together to keep from saying more.

"While you were prancing around, Paradise Massage was robbed at gunpoint. Didn't you hear the gunshot?"

"I certainly was not prancing around! Are you all right? Was anyone hurt?" She looked him over with concern. The rain slicker was too hot and confining, buttoned up so tight. Her face flushed from heat and stress. Other than dusty, he looked unhurt. She brushed a cobweb from his shoulder and their glances met. She swallowed hard, understanding the true meaning of being hot under the collar.

"I don't think so. I had to crawl across the attic to get out. Promised my masseuse hush money. She's going to meet me at Tim Horton's in a few minutes. And that reminds me—I should move the truck, in case we've been spotted."

She pressed her lips together and climbed into the passenger side. He started up the vehicle and drove a few blocks, making a few twists and turns, then pulled into a parking stall at the coffee shop. He withdrew his wallet from his pants pocket and counted out five hundred dollar bills, folding them in half.

"So, did you learn anything? Plant the bugs?" he asked as she remained silent, her lips pressed together.

"Yes, I planted two bugs. One in the ladies' bathroom and one in the office, filling out an employment application. But, if we're going to be working together, we need to lay some ground rules." She seethed inside but took the time to enunciate each syllable as though she was talking to an imbecile, which was what he had just been.

He turned his dark gaze her way. "No time for that. But I will say that I can't have you disobeying procedure, leaving yourself open to harm. I don't need that worry on top of all the other shit that's going down right now."

"I'll give you that a lot of shit's going on. But I can handle myself. I did before you came to town, and I will after you leave." Why did that feel so discomforting? Hell, she'd just met him and he wasn't easy. "I've discovered there's an upcoming war with the triad, which is probably what was behind the robbery at Paradise."

"Yes, I discovered that as well and I was able to place bugs." He drummed his fingers on the steering wheel. They were well-shaped, strong and tanned. Was the rest of him so fine? According to her dreams, yes. But dreams aren't the same as real life. She had a stab of envy for the young woman who had just laid hands on him. The sweet odor of coconut filled the cab, making her frown. Exactly how far had they gone in that massage room?

"There she is," he said. Gabby looked out of the windshield and spotted a stunning petite young woman hurrying across the parking lot, headed for the side door of the coffee shop. She rolled her eyes. Of course, she'd be drop-dead gorgeous.

"You wait here." She was about to protest when his next statement made too much sense to protest. "I don't want your involvement exposed. Not yet."

"Fine, but hurry. The clock's ticking."

He grunted. "You think I don't know that? And if you're too hot, I have a T-shirt in the backseat."

She raised her eyebrows. "What?"

"You're flushed red. It's not good for you."

She grimaced and he walked across the parking lot. *Nice ass, goddamn it all to hell.* She unbuckled and rummaged around in the back, finding the tee, and got busy changing out of the hot rain slicker, tugging the shirt down over her head. It caught in her bun and pulled her hair down as well, pins springing out and pinging on the dash and floor. Annoyed, she tided the thick mass best she could then sat back to wait. Cole's fragrance filled her nostrils as it wafted from the material and she took a deep breath in, finding his scent arousing. *Spicy and sex as hell, just like the guy. Damn it.*

She checked her messages. Her sister had sent a text, asking how her new job was going. She got busy answering, fingers flying over the keys. She needed to tell somebody.

Never guess who I'm working with? Guy from last night. Real FUBAR

No FW!!!

Yes way. Talk later. On the job.

As she looked back up, a trio of young men pulled up in a black car with tinted windows, music blaring, drawing attention. They appeared to be looking for someone as they made their drive by, black and red bandanas tied either around their necks or across their foreheads. A sense of foreboding overcame her and she reached for the door handle.

* * * *

Day Three: 1:57 p.m.

Cole got his coffee black and joined the woman at a table, glancing around, checking to see if any of the customers could be a potential threat. It was a typical Tim Horton's coffee shop with a line for ordering food and coffee, the round café tables going unfilled for the most part as people used the drive-in option more. But he didn't like the location of the table she'd chosen—he couldn't see the vehicle. Or Gabby.

"Let's move over there." He pointed toward the opposite side of the coffee shop. She didn't say anything, but picked up her brown Styrofoam cup. He gave her a hand up off the chair and slipped the cache of folded money hidden in his palm into her hand.

She gave him a smile of satisfaction and followed him across the room. Cole kept the truck in the edge of his vision as he sipped his hot coffee, the fresh fragrance of the beverage invigorating, trying to think of something to say to the young woman. He needed to handle this operation delicately, use anything he could discover in the course of the conversation that might give him an edge.

"You come to Chinatown often?" she asked, making him rack his brain for the best possible excuse that would also curry favor.

"Yes, I spend time in the area, trying to drum up business."

"What business you in?"

"I have a company on the side that sells watches, jewelry, purses, stuff like that. Very good quality, good as the real thing." The area was notorious for contraband goods. In fact, most goods sold were knock-offs of the real thing. It was how most of the merchants made their living.

"You can get me fancy stuff for lower cost?" she asked, running the tip of her tongue over her bottom lip with interest. He felt like a real shit, leading her on.

She seemed like such a nice girl too, hard-working, and she had helped him out of a bad situation. He owed her something. Hell, he could have been killed. And, if what he suspected was true, she was stuck in a dead-end job for the foreseeable future, and he would bet she'd be paying off for years to come the costs of being brought to Canada. His heart squeezed with sympathy for her plight and so many other young people just wanting a chance at the Canadian dream. A decent life that provided for their family back home. So many broke their spirits trying to obtain it, held by so often by their own people. Fucking unfair. And it didn't make him feel one iota better knowing he was using her as well—she could be a useful source, going forward.

"Sure? What do you want?"

"Anything really." She shrugged. "All girls love jewelry and purses. Very nice to have. Make nice gifts for when I need and I can also sell them. Help you. Help me. Pearl is my name. What yours?"

"I'm Cole. I'll get some nice things together for you to check out, if you like."

She gave him a demure smile and a small nod, eyes downcast, though it was obvious she was pleased. Christ, she was a real sweetheart. Sure, she didn't hold a candle to Gabby, but that was a given. No one did.

"You're good at your job, Pearl," he complimented her, rubbing the back of his neck. "I feel much more relaxed." Not quite true. Worry over Gabby had stripped that away ASAP. Pearl smiled, though, making him feel a bit less like a shit-heel.

He caught movement near the truck and turned to find Gabby had gotten out and was marching across the pavement. *What the fuck?* But, before he could react, a loud series of bangs rang out. He ducked down in his seat, peering through the glass. The sharp scent of gunpowder drifted in the front door as it was opened, letting in smoky residue. He squinted through the mist, his eyes watering. Then he was up and running to the entrance.

Where was she?

He looked around in fear, his heart thundering. He spotted her lying on the pavement a few feet from the entrance. He raced to her side, desperate to see if she was injured. If they had hurt her, he'd tear them limb from limb.

"I'm fine. It was just fireworks. A warning from what I think are rival gang members. They were dressed in triad colors, black and red bandanas tied around their foreheads," she blurted out as he helped her to her feet, making sure she wasn't bleeding anywhere.

"Thank God," he said, pulling her into his arms, able to breathe now that the danger had passed. She felt so good as he held her tiny body tight to his, making him aware of how well her curves fitted into the hollows of his muscular frame and how amazing the fragrance was wafting off her warm flesh, heated from the adrenaline surging through her veins. All flowery with a hint of feminine musk underneath like burnt sugar. His cock responded, growing hard in an instant. She didn't pull away from the evidence, but pushed up against him. He couldn't have pulled away now if his life had depended on it.

It was only the sound of a woman's raised voice that broke the moment. "You meet me later? Give me what you promised?" Pearl asked, frowning while looking at them both. Under her intent perusal, he took a step back from Gabby, taking charge of the situation. He prayed his hard-on wasn't obvious, painful as it was pressing against his zipper. He wanted to keep Pearl's cooperation, no matter the cost.

"Yes, I will be in touch," he said, his voice raspy and hoarse. He cleared his throat, wishing away the ache in his balls. What the fuck had just happened?

"How? You need my number?" she asked, proving she did not want to miss out on anything. And as uncomfortable as the situation was, she wasn't giving up.

He nodded and took out his phone. Keyed in the numbers she recited.

"See you later. Bye." Pearl walked away. *Finally.*

He turned to give Gabby a look, but she was already gone. He followed and got in behind the wheel.

The throb still demanding between her legs shocked Gabby as she buckled up the seatbelt. Her blood was pulsing under her skin, her flesh on fire. *I want nothing more than to fuck this man.* The idea left her breathless. Pressed up against him, she had been far too aware of his powerful arms, his flat stomach, his chiseled pecs and his huge cock pressing against her, demanding entry. *Fuck.* It must have been the adrenaline from the shock. She swallowed, not ready to look his way, instead peering out of the side window as if the view was the most fascinating ever. And what was the deal with Pearl? The color green surging around the edges of Gabby's vision only added to her confusion.

"So." Cole cleared his throat. "Where do we go from here?"

Good fucking question. How about the closest motel? Or better, yet your place or mine. Or perhaps you would like to explain about Pearl? Just what the fuck is going down with her? Is that the kind of girl you want? Instead she managed to squeak out some words, gaining some control. "I think we should head back to home base. Share what's happened and what we know."

"Of course." He started the truck, turning around to check the space behind them, giving her a quick look. "But later, tonight, I want to spend time with you. Keep you and me on the same page. Okay? Talk about our day."

"Talk, eh?" she said with a snort of laughter, teasing him. Hell, her clit was still vibrating and aching like it thought it was her last chance on earth for a good fuck. She snuck a glance his way.

He had clamped his lips shut, driving out of the parking lot and back to TETRAD as if he couldn't get there fast enough. *Boy, sure get that.* It might not have been her first rodeo, but it was the first time she hadn't cared that anyone was watching her rub herself all over a male of the species. She flushed hot just thinking about it. Oh, this was going well. And on the job, too. A job she wanted to keep in the worst way. She shook her head in dismay, not liking the complication of a man who was a magnet, who seemed to fire off electrons in her on a cellular level that defied reason. She sighed. *Going to be a long week spent in such enthralling company, and hell on earth not to act on it.*

* * * *

They couldn't pull up in front of the business fast enough in Gabby's opinion. She was praying Silk was available. She needed to lay this on someone before she came apart at the seams. She left Cole to make his own way inside, racing for the front door when she spied Silk's head through the glass. *Thank God.*

85

"Hey, Silk, you busy? I really need to talk."

Silk's eyes grew wide as her friend almost jumped on her, tugging her into a side office and shutting out the world.

"My goodness, what's going on? Something happen?" Silk sat and gestured for her to join her. But Gabby was too full of adrenaline and hormones and had to keep pacing. She thought better on her feet, anyway.

"Nothing's happened, at least nothing more than some fireworks thrown by some triad gangers. But that's not it, not the problem," Gabby began, thrusting her hands into her hair and scraping it back from her face and neck, far too warm.

"What is the problem?"

"It's Cole. I don't know if I can work with that man. He's such a distraction and he doesn't trust me, I just know it! He's been questioning my ability, right?"

Silk had the grace to blush. "He doesn't know you. When he does, he'll come around. Trust me."

"I feel so under the gun here. If I can't even be trusted to do my job, go into the difficult places, like you did in LA, then what the fuck! He's driving me crazy. You know that? Coming onto massage girls, promising them God knows what." Gabby's exasperation grew with each word she spoke. Afraid she was going to go too far and spoil her chances at keeping her new job, she clamped her mouth shut and sat across from her friend.

"Ah, he's been doing his job. That does suck."

"What? His job is to flirt, get massages and drink coffee with bimbos?"

"You know what I mean. Working on getting intel, setting up contacts. Smart. Won't you say? Wouldn't you be willing to take one for the team if it helped the situation?"

"Sure. Of course. But this is different."

"Only thing different is it's harder for Cole than for most. I don't know if I should tell you this, but I think you need to see a clearer picture of what you're dealing with here. I think you're very attracted to the man and you're not seeing things clearly enough to do your job well. I want you to become an important part of this team, I know you can do that, Gabby, but you need to understand some things about Cole. What he's been through this past few years."

Silk stopped and grabbed a bottle of water from the desk, twisted the cap off and took a long swallow. She gave Gabby a steady look then seemed to decide something. "What's happened to him would have taken most men down, sent them right out of their freakin' minds. And it did for him, as well, for a time. Then he pulled himself up by his bootstraps, for his son Mathew, wanting to honor him by helping others in dire need. That's why this case cuts him so deeply, being a kidnapping. His own son was snatched, stolen from a playground two years ago, never to be seen again. Then, less than a year ago his wife died of an overdose. We're not sure if it was suicide or not, but it came down to the same thing. Cole found her, in the bathroom of their house, but it already was too late. She was gone."

Gabby sat, too stunned to speak. Her thoughts froze on an image of a son who looked like Cole vanishing, never to be seen again. A parent's worst nightmare. *My God.* To think of what he'd lost, and he was still standing, still trying to do the right thing. And she was calling him on a bit of harmless flirting, making his life harder. Shame filled her. Colored her world.

She took a deep breath. Let it out in a slow stream of air.

"I had no idea," she said at last, looking at Silk with regret. She swallowed. Hot tears filled her eyes but she swept away with the back of her hand. Tears couldn't fix this one.

"He doesn't like to talk about it. Too painful. But this case, with Sara missing, this has be cutting him to the bone and I'm telling now you so that you will be aware—stay sensitive to this issue. We're all worried for him. But he'll have none of it. You know, typical guy stuff, insisting on handling everything on his own. Says it's no one else's burden to carry. Insists on doing what needs to be done. And he does do that. And I get it. I would, too. I can't even go there—to imagine the world of pain if anything happened...to our son."

Silk drew a breath, swiping away tears, as well. "What he must have gone through, must still be in. Just give him a break. That's all I ask. He's a good man who's been through more than any of us can even imagine. Things none of us ever, ever, want to imagine."

Gabby grabbed a water bottle and took a couple of long pulls. She threw the empty container into the recycling bin, hitting it square on.

"One more thing," Silk said, finishing with her own water and adding to the bin, as well. "Please don't let on to Cole. He hates people knowing his business. Hates people feeling sorry for him. It could make things worse between the two of you."

"Not sure that's possible," Gabby answered, wishing somehow they could rewind the last twenty-four hours, begin again. *But life isn't like that, it's not a dress rehearsal. No, it's a stark, wild, in-your-face adventure, and one to be ready for and do what's asked or be knocked out of the way.* Didn't she know that all too well.

* * * *

Day Three: 7:34 p.m.

Cole's phone buzzed in his pocket while he was walking back to the reception area from debriefing Quinn. Minute-by-minute detail and analysis was always crucial to any important case. And with the increased stakes of this case, no detail could be left unstudied. Cole shook his head and slid the phone out, checking the number. *Finally.*

"Got to see someone—alone. I'll be back asap," he said with a nod in Gabby's direction as he caught sight of her just leaving Silk's office, her friend right behind her. He frowned, narrowing his eyes, certain Gabby's held a telltale pink around the edges. He glanced at Silk. Hers were the same. What the fuck was going on?

"'An army marches on its stomach'," Gabby quipped, striding over as if she were covering something up with fake camaraderie.

"Sorry?" he asked. Was she back to being an air-head? Then he felt guilty, having spent time watching how competent she could be.

"Napoleon Bonaparte. I think he might have known something about it. And I'm coming with." He was about to object when she held her hand up. "I can wait in the truck while you talk with him. It will save time." She had to know who he was going to see and he couldn't argue, because she was right. She picked up a couple of the cellophane-wrapped sandwiches from the cooler where Silk had deposited them earlier, and some water. Silk knew the drill. Keep food handy for when people have time to grab it.

"Silk, can you let Jake and Quinn know the deal?" Cole asked.

"Sure thing. Good luck. We need Satoshi onboard. Offer what you have to."

He nodded. "Whatever it takes."

He held the door open for Gabby and hurried after her. She climbed in and placed the food on the back seat while he slammed the vehicle in gear, heading south down Granville Street, driving toward the pre-arranged meeting place. Always the same and easy to remember — the largest cemetery in town.

"What's the deal with Satoshi?" Gabby asked. Discombobulated in Cole's company didn't cover it. Knowing what she knew now, she could never go back. Her body thrummed, even more aware of his presence than before.

"Excuse me?" Cole tensed, turning and giving her a quick glance.

"Just wondering how you guys met? Heck, people have been looking to discover his real identity for years. No one seems to know who he is and yet you not only know him, but you're his friend."

"I wouldn't call us close friends, exactly, more like similar-minded men, but we do go back a ways. We met at university." He threaded his way through noon-hour traffic, his eyes troubled. Gabby fought the urge to let on she knew anything. She had to play this right or she would never forgive herself for causing him more pain.

"How are you doing with this case? I know it's a hard one. A friend's child is missing," she asked, needing to find out something about how his situation without giving herself away. Something about how his mind worked.

He narrowed his eyes, giving her a suspicious glance. "Fine. I don't want to talk about it. Not going to help knowing anything about our 'feelings'. Only thing that helps is action. Agreed? At least until Sara's home." His voice was sharp, an unexpected rebuke.

She swallowed. "Yeah, I hear you." She'd wanted to reach out, do something about the rawness of what she'd learned, but circumstances had curtailed it. She took a deep breath, keeping her gaze focused out of the window.

When they turned into the Mountain View Cemetery, she looked over at Cole in surprise. "You're meeting him here?"

"Yeah, whatever city I'm in, I just locate the largest cemetery and the oldest graves," he said with a shrug as he parked.

"It's a beautiful spot, I'll give you that," she replied, watching a man walking his dog down one of the well-maintained paths.

"Been here before?" he asked turning and grabbing a water from the backseat. His fragrance wafted between them and she breathed it in with pleasure. Fucking intoxicating about summed it up.

"Not in a while. But my grandparents are buried here. If I had known we'd be coming here, I would have brought flowers."

He uncapped the water, taking a long swig, then swiping his hand over his mouth.

"You should eat something," she said, unable to stop herself.

"Who are you, my mother?" he said, snorting.

"I don't ever want to be your mother!" she ground out through gritted teeth, fire exploding in her belly. That was the last fucking thing she wanted.

"What do you want?" he growled, flinging the words out, a definite challenge, the call of the wild in the darkness.

She swallowed hard, thinking of all the things she did want. Wanted him to take her in his arms, wanted him to kiss her, caress her. She licked her lips. Was she going to survive this mess without a meltdown?

Lust permeated the air. How could he not notice when it was rising off her in waves?

"I want us to get along better if we're going to spend time together." That sounded reasonable enough to her ears.

He turned to her, a dark warrior, his expression almost menacing in its intensity. As if he had to do something he was fighting with all his might not to do.

"Okay." He gave a huge sigh and cleared his throat. "For what it's worth, I'm sorry. I didn't mean to bark at you. None of this is your fault. It's been a trying day and it's only noon."

His apology surprised her.

"No worries. I shouldn't have bothered you about something so trivial with all we have on our plates. Not eating for a few days won't hurt me, anyway. I've got a pair of hips that will certainly agree with that diagnosis." She gave a rueful grin.

"What!" He shot her a look of disbelief. "You're perfect as you are. Absolutely perfect."

Their eyes locked. She was lost then, reaching out to him the exact moment he reached out for her. Their lips collided, sparks sizzling along sensitive nerve endings, lighting up the universe within. His lips commanded, crushing her mouth, forcing it open, his tongue swirling to discover her. Senses reeling, she pushed against him, hungry, tasting him, insatiable. He reached for her breasts with both hands, cupping their new-found heaviness, seeking the nipples that grew instantly hard under his firm, oh-so-perfect touch.

She moaned, the heat inside about to combust. Her head swam with the sensations. *Who cares if someone discovers us? I want this man. Now.*

And still he kissed her, ravaging her mouth, raining kisses onto her lips, her cheeks, her neck and finally the tops of her breasts. He pulled up her T-shirt, seeking the naked flesh. Hungry, unable to stop, she encouraged him, arching her back, wanting his lips on her at this second more than life itself. Wanting all her clothes to disappear.

She dropped her hand to his lap, discovering his cock hard against his zipper. Another moan. From him this time. She caressed him, encouraged him, wanting him to throw caution to the wind. Make love to her right there, in broad daylight.

A buzz sounded, pulling her from wherever she had gone, lost in a sea of lust. *What? No. Not now.* Cole's phone was vibrating in his pocket. Insistent.

He stilled, as if he, too, was waking up from a trance. His warmth left her as he let her go to answer it. She tugged her clothes back into some semblance of order. Pressing her hand to her mouth, she discovered she was trembling all over. Hot and cold. And damn needy.

"He's here." His voice sounded odd. She didn't trust herself to speak, but only nodded.

He gave her a nod, climbed out and walked away. She watched, eyes wide open. A narrow escape. Give it another minute and they would have been at it like a pair of rabbits in the field. God, what had she been thinking? She flushed and took a few slow breaths. *Well, this just got a whole lot more complicated.*

'Satoshi' was sitting on a bench near the oldest graves located in Mountain View under a large shade tree. Acres of small plots surrounded his still figure, many dotted with green bushes and sprays of color. He had a ball cap pulled low on his forehead, the ubiquitous sunglasses in place. And he was not Asian but a blond-haired Swede with his hair tied into a low ponytail. 'Satoshi' was the cover of this man, the inventor of universal money — a new money created by computers. A money better than gold and easier to transport, though like gold, it still required work to release it — computational work. And with a digital security key, available at a click of a mouse, not needing armed guards to keep it safe. A tall, thin, idealistic and very particular kind of man, he sat with his long limbs draped over the bench, his languid pose hiding a mind like quicksilver. He missed nothing. He didn't turn toward Cole, but just gestured at the view.

"Think when my turn comes, I'll chose this place. Nice and peaceful. And yet people come through here all the time, giving it life. Rather a hopeful place, if a cemetery can be thought of that way."

"Didn't take you for a romantic, Nils." Cole slipped onto the bench beside him.

"How are you doing? Long time since you've been in touch." Nils turned and gave him a look, one hard to read through the dark glasses.

"Yeah, I'm sorry about that. A lot of crap was coming down." The nerves in his stomach twisted with memory.

"I was sorry to hear about your wife and son. I wish you had gotten in touch sooner. I would have spent time, you know, helping where I could."

"Thanks." Cole pushed through the instant pain that threatened to engulf him. What was happening with Gabby was making him reel as well. *God, why are you putting such temptation in my way now, of all times?* "But I need your help right now. A young girl's missing and the kidnappers want something almost impossible to achieve. And you're the only one who can do it. The only one who knows how bitcoin was source coded and can hack in, leaving no trail to the original software. Siphon off funds to an account. And we only got five days to manage it. Or Sara stays missing."

"Who's got her?" Nils stared into the distance.

"Asian gang, BTK, Born To Kill, we believe. Just in the process of confirming it and finding out their plans. Bugged both their known establishments this morning."

"And in three days you expect me to hand over the code that will make billions for criminals? You've got to be kidding me. Think of all the damage they can do with that kind of funding. The criminal enterprises that will flourish!"

"You can't let a young girl pay the price for our mistakes. Christ, Nils. Look at her." Cole pulled out his phone and filled the screen with Sara's innocent face. She was laughing at something, her eyes alight, her sleek dark hair flowing around her slender shoulders. A heartbreaker who was so beautiful.

Nils let out a protracted sigh. "Do you know how many people have tried to blackmail me?" he asked, his tone harsh and unyielding.

"But, surely, you can see your way to help just this one child? Think of what you're doing. How can you live with yourself if you don't? Help the one right in front of you. You have to!"

"No buts. My father always said everything after the word but's bullshit, anyway. I cannot do what you ask. I'm sorry. Many more will suffer if I do than just one child." He shook his head, his expression grim, his mind seeming made up. Desperate, he racked his brain.

"Fuck! No! You can't turn away from this, Nils. You created this mess with all your ideology about keeping big government out of our affairs. You have to fix this!"

Silence. He tried to calm down, but his heart was racing too fast, slamming against his rib cage. If he failed here, he didn't know what he would do. His whole life looked to implode again and it hurt more than words could say.

"For what it's worth, I am truly sorry," Nils began, his eyes taking on a further burden. "I know this must cut to the bone, Cole, but damn it, I wasn't the one who kidnapped that child and is blackmailing the family. And if I was to do such a thing, ever create and release special source code, the flood gates would open. You know that. No. I just can't do it. If you say fuck the future, it's guaranteed to fuck you. It goes against all that I stand for. Perhaps get them to see reason. Do what everyone else does in the bitcoin hacker world — a quick smash and grab. It's worked a few times. Worth a try."

Cole stood, defeated, his brain reeling with an anguish he tried to hide. *Think.* But he had no more persuasive cards in his arsenal.

Nils stood. "Okay. I hope in time you can see past this, that we can remain friends. That you will see I was right. Go after them. Fight these men on their home turf. Do what you do best."

Cole straightened, his resolve strengthening. They were on their own now. "A pretty speech isn't going to fix this or bring Sara home," he said, bitterness lacing his words.

Nils winced. Cole knew it wasn't his fault, but his refusal to help hurt. Big-time.

"I know you're upset, I admit I would be too. But I have to stand firm. There's a thin line between good and evil these days — thinner than it's ever been. I can't cross it, even for you."

Cole heard the release of anger in his tone. "That's it, then."

Nils grimaced, his lips pressed into a thin line. This was costing him as well.

Cole walked away slowly in the direction of the truck, trying to see past his next move of planning a bug in the men's room at Chang's. When he caught sight of Gabby's face through the windshield, he gave her a single shake of his head.

He joined her in the cab, his eyes drawn to her lovely face, pain lancing him when he found it filled with worry, a sharp crease burrowing between her eyebrows while she chewed on her lips. The lips he had lost himself in only moments ago. It seemed like forever now, the sight a pure aphrodisiac. He reached over and drew her to him, rougher than he intended. Took that beautiful concerned face between the palms of his hand

and claimed a kiss of those perfect pink lips. The effect startling, satisfying, essential, the electrical current between them bursting into flames.

He pressed harder, seeking the warmth within. His blood heated red-hot, coursing under his skin, tightening his cock until it felt about to burst free from his jeans, hard as steel. A moan. A gasp. The outside world dropped away, making only this moment, this second, all that mattered.

She softened into him across the annoyance of the center partition between the seats. He wanted to drag her right up close to him, push into her, fill her with himself. He was lost in her, grasping a full breast and finding the nipple hard, budded. The warmth of the pliant flesh sent him reeling. God, he wanted her. Wanted to have her stretched naked beneath him, wet for him. Wanted into the very core of her. *Make me forget.*

"Fuck, woman," he murmured against her lips, "I have to have you. Now." Their breaths mingled, heating the air around them, obscuring the outside world as moisture formed, clouding over the windows. It ran down the glass in rivets, like the tears of the world.

His hands pulled at her clothing until she began to help, shucking off her shoes, jeans and panties in one frantic movement. He unbuckled his belt and pulled down the zipper, yanked a condom from his pocket. She tore it from his hands and before he could get his jeans and boxers completely off, she was on top of him, centering herself over him, grasping his cock with one hand, rolling the condom on and thrusting him into her pussy. He slid inside, pushing past the slick, tight entrance to thrust up into her, pulling her down as far as he could, burying himself balls-deep inside her tight warmth.

"Oh, my God," he moaned, his cock straining for sweet release, his head swimming with the quickness of being inside her. He'd dreamed of this moment since he'd first laid eyes on her. He lunged into her, burying his face in her fragrant hair, working his hands over her naked breasts, pushing her bra cups down to make them jut out farther until she moaned against his mouth, wetness flooding her channel.

His body wasn't his own, his need powerful. He forgot everything else, where they were, what was going on. He was rough, rougher than he had ever been with a woman. His hot cum rushed up from inside his balls, tingling and seeking release. Raw. Like he had never known. Harder than he had ever been.

"I'm coming—" he growled, tugging on her nipples, reaching down and rubbing on her swollen clit, wanting her to reach orgasm with him.

He sucked one tightly budded nipple into his mouth, drawing hard and eliciting more sweet moans. He took a deep breath, his lungs about to burst as he forgot to breathe. The fragrance of sex filled the cab, their odors mingling.

"I'm almost there," she shouted, slamming herself down on to him over and over, her breasts bouncing with each impact, her pussy squeezing him tight. A final thrust and they collapsed against each other, into each other, breath harsh and resounding in the confining space.

An alarm went off nearby, blasting through the thick moisture-laden air. He reached around Gabby and turned off the offending electronics, the action causing her reddened breasts to press up against his chest. He felt her heartbeat, precious life coursing through her body, sending signals right back down to his cock. *Sweet Jesus, help me, I want her again. Right now.* He grabbed hold of himself with great difficulty, coming out of the madness that had descended. He remembered where they were and regret stung his soul. What the hell had he been thinking? "I'm sorry. I shouldn't have done that. Fuck, this isn't the time or place for this. This is wrong on so many levels."

Gabby looked at him, the same height as him on his lap. Her eyes searched his, their depths bluer and the gold speckles shinning. She swallowed. He wanted to kiss his way down that slim column again, kiss every square inch of her. *In a proper bed.* He pressed his lips together. He'd forgotten himself, forgotten that this was impossible. He could never take that chance again. Never let a woman in too close. And all his instincts screamed that Gabby would be that one, if anyone could. He had to protect her. From himself.

Chapter Five

Day Three: 9:12 p.m.

A line had just been crossed and realization hit Gabby, hard. *Can't take it back now.* She stared into Cole's soulful brown eyes as he expressed his regret without needing to say a word, his cock still hard within her as she straddled his lap, the evidence still apparent between them.

Cole had wanted this as much as she did. She had no regrets for having jumped on him. Lust had overtaken them. The heat and passion she could see in his eyes, feel in his body, touch if she but reached down between her legs and grasped where their bodies joined into one, all had screamed his need. Her need.

Now, he was pulling away. Mentally, if not physically. Of course, he was right. Not the time nor place. But still, hurtful. And wanting each other, it wasn't that wrong, certainly not the federal case he was making of it. But she should have known better. *This kind of thing only leads to heartache. Fuck, Gabby, get your mind back on the case. It might even be easier now to do that with insta-lust out of the way. Maybe...*

"Ah, I have to move," she said. He grasped her waist and helped her back into her seat as easy as if she were a child. His strength astonished her. It was an advantage, when she thought of her weak weasel of an ex. Weak in every way. *Damn, don't go there,* she cautioned herself. *Enjoy one moment for a change.* She donned her panties and jeans, rearranging her bra and T-shirt.

Just breathe. In and out. She swiped at the passenger window with her forearm. The moisture at least had blocked the view. She caught sight of an eagle wheeling in the somber gray sky above the graveyard of tombs and trees and flowered paths, this whispering oasis in the heart of Vancouver. The sight of the magnificent bird eased her. Centered her. And didn't it portent good luck? Seeing an eagle?

"Okay. If you're ready, we'd better check in with the others. Tell them what's occurred and see what's next," Cole said, as if nothing had happened, as if their whole world hadn't changed.

"Fine." She crossed her arms over her chest, sitting up straighter, keeping her tone ice-cold. She was suddenly angry for some reason. "Let's go."

"Gabby—"

"It's okay, I get it. This is wrong, on every level." She threw the words back at him.

"I didn't mean it quite like that. I mean—hell, I don't know what I meant." His expression tightened. *Damn, rejection hurts.*

When he said nothing, staring out of the front windshield, she straightened up in the seat. "Could you take me back to my place? I need a quick shower."

He nodded, staying silent, and had her back to her townhouse in record time by nearly breaking the speed limits.

"You're welcome to come inside and clean up as well," she offered throwing the idea out there, unbuckling her seatbelt.

"Best I wait here." The terse words hurt. So much for a quick tryst in the shower. Afraid of embarrassing herself, she rushed from the truck and into the brownstone, slamming the door behind her.

Cole hit the steering wheel with his hands, full-on, sending pain jarring up his forearms. What was he going to do about this impossible situation? He'd taken advantage of Gabby, an inexcusable action. His very own clusterfuck. And now they would both pay the price. His cell phone rang and when he saw the number, he groaned aloud. *Why the fuck now?* He made a quick decision. Didn't answer it then felt like a failure for not being the bigger brother. Without realizing what he was going to do, he called the number back.

Beau began speaking before he could say a word. "Cole. I'm in town on business. I'm at the airport and I need to see you. And hell, maybe I can help with your case." Cole could hear the muffled sounds of a loudspeaker in the background and people milling about. *Fuck, why now, why today?*

Gabby climbed back into the passenger side as he closed his eyes tightly, trying to find the patience to answer Beau. Her fresh fragrance drifted over him in a soft cloud, stirring his cock to full attention in one second. He forced his mind off what he had just missed out on – Gabby naked and wet – and tried to formulate some words.

"It would be better if you didn't do that, Beau. Just go and check into a hotel. There's nothing really for you to do. We've got it covered. TETRAD has all the help it needs. But thanks for the offer. And sorry about this, but I have to go." Cole hung up. This day just kept getting better and better.

"Who was that?" Gabby asked, giving him a speculative look, looking all composed from her time inside the townhouse. The peach-colored blouse she wore suited her, bringing out the pink in her lips. Lips he would never kiss again if he was smart. But right now, he felt anything but smart.

"No one."

"Sounded like someone." Her inquisitive tone annoyed him for some reason.

"What's your problem?"

"*My* problem?" Her voice rose a complete octave as she turned to stare at him, a belligerent expression coloring her fair complexion bright pink. "I'm not the one hiding in plain sight."

"I'm not hiding, I'm right here, for fuck's sake." He took a full breath. "Okay, that was my brother. Beauregard. Beau. We don't get along very well."

"Why not?"

He grunted. "Other than he's relapsed back into drugs twice after a spell in rehab, broke our parents' hearts and stole anything not nailed down to support his habit, not a damn thing."

"Is he clean now?"

"Says he is." Cole shrugged. "But he'd better not get in the way this week. Sara needs our best efforts. He'll just have to wait until I clear the decks if he wants to catch up."

"You are right about that—Sara does need our best efforts. You know, Cole, if there is ever anything you want or need to talk about, I'm a good listener."

"Why would I need to talk?" he shot back, the old anger surging before shame lanced him. He started the truck's engine, placing it in gear in preparation for pulling away from the curb. None of his previous life was Gabby's fault. No, it was all on him. His burden to carry. Alone.

Gabby's cell phone rang and she glanced at the caller ID. *Jake.* Good, maybe he had something.

"Gabby, we've got new intel from the bug in the café. It's definitely BTK and it looks like something huge is going to go down with the triad, gang saber-rattling shit. The bastards were careful, not giving much away, but I wanted you to know so you're aware of the danger you're in. You don't want to get caught in the crossfire."

"Good. What's the group's strategy for dealing with sensitive intel like this? Do you have a guy on the inside?" Gabby needed to know. "Want us to swing by HQ?" she asked. *Please. I want to exchange my partner.*

"Yes, we have a guy, and no, no need to come in. How did your partner make out with his guy?" No names on phones. First rule of operation. And she was stuck for the foreseeable future with the torment of Cole. If only he'd didn't smell so fucking good or look so damn hot, she could manage this a whole lot easier. Of course, now he smelled like her, giving her a flashback of how he'd gotten that way. Mind on job, Gabby.

"I'll let him tell you." She held her cell phone to Cole's ear. Let him deal with it.

With a few terse words, he filled Jake in.

She dared a look at him as he drove. About as shut down as a man could manage. Hell, it hadn't been that bad, had it, fucking in the truck? Not like he hadn't been a willing participant. And asking about his caller? Yeah, not such good form.

She put her phone to back to her ear. "Gabby here."

"Okay, I want you to head back to Chinatown. Keep an eye on Chang, stay with him. I'll send you some photos Quinn took of known gang members today," Jake instructed.

"Good, we're heading there now."

She hung up on the call, speaking to the windshield. "Jake wants us in Chinatown to keep an eye on Chang and his crew. It's been confirmed he's our guy. Intel from the bug in the café."

"Good. Check in the back. I brought two sets of earbuds so we can listen in on the conversations while we're in the field. They hook up to the portals in the console."

She rummaged around on the back seat, located the necessary equipment and deposited the items on her lap, buckling herself back in. "When we get back to the office, we should ask to change partners. Maybe *you* can hire someone. Make this thing easier for you."

As soon as she said the words, she wanted to snatch them back. She was only drawing attention to something she wanted to go away. She hooked into the impressive onsite computer system Cole had installed in a large section of the passenger side of the dash, having taken out the glove boxes and CD player. There were more fancy gadgets than she knew the use for. *Figures, definitely a guy thing.* She could only imagine how a tech guy's brain worked when it was fueled by imagination. And an unlimited budget. Jake was blessed with old family money.

"Gabby, I'm sorry. You don't understand."

"Oh, I think I do."

"Yeah, do you get that I'm half-crazy with wanting to be with you? Do you get that I've been fighting the attraction tooth and nail since I first met you? That it's the most insane time of all for this crap to be going down? Do you really get that? And being with you, being inside you, I don't have the words, but, it was the most amazing thing."

His explosion of words stunned her. Both of them, if Cole's horrified expression was anything to go by. To have a man like him admit such a thing went against all she had known in the past. And his anguish was real. It was written all over his face. Undeniably. She realized now he did not take what they had shared lightly.

"Uh, no, I didn't quite get all that." She swallowed hard. Now she felt like a bigger fool. "We should talk about this later. You're right. This isn't the time or place." Anger had been replaced by surprise and relief. He did want her. As much as she wanted him. She should lighten things between them or the next days would prove unbearable. She chose to be the voice of reason.

"I will say this—it isn't an all-or-nothing kind of thing. People connect and disconnect all the time. You know, deal with their lust and move on. I'm a big-city girl. I can handle it." *In a bug's eye.* But never again was she going to let a man know how drawn she was to him, even as she felt relieved he was feeling it too.

"I'm not like that—I don't do one-night stands. It's harder for me than you, I guess, I'm a few years older than you, nearly a different generation. Thirty-three. How old are you? Twenty, twenty-one?"

"Twenty-five," she rebuked. "An eight-year difference does *not* count in the scheme of things."

"No, that's a chunk of time, eight full years of experience separating us. A world of difference, with the kind of life I've led. You don't know me. Oh, hell, I don't know what I believe, anymore. Let's just leave this thing alone for now." His words stunned her further, but she had just brought them on herself, suggesting it was a lark when she knew it was not. *Why did I give him that stupid impression?*

"Fine," she lied. It was far from fine. This was uncharted territory for her. She'd never had a man admit to such a thing or talk like Cole was communicating with her. *Raw and real. And never have I wanted to impress a man more, damn it.* A text message announced its presence just as the video console surveillance monitoring system built-in to the dash buzzed, pulling her instantly away from her thoughts. She checked the message.

"An alert. TETRAD's sending us intel and photos of some of Chang's crew to the monitor," she said, bringing up the screen on the built-in video and listening device created and designed by Cole to aid in surveillance in the field. They carefully studied each face, forgetting everything else. They needed to be able to identify them. Time to go to work.

Cole continued driving and a few minutes later was heading under the Millennium Gate, perched over Pender Street and welcoming everyone since 2002. The tightly packed shops and businesses that made up Chinatown created an odd sense of going backward in time, a historical and cultural oasis existing within metropolitan Vancouver that incomers from more modern cities found somewhat jarring, Gabby knew. She wondered if Cole might come to enjoy the district's charm—at some point in the future. Not that she wanted him to stick around.

Parking a few businesses down from Chang's Café, he said, "I'm going inside and order something. Get a sense of the place. You wait here. You've already been seen once today. A second time might look suspicious. And, Gabby, please, keep an eye out—with this gang war about to heat up, things can take a nasty turn at any time. Triad and BTK are notorious enemies. Who knows what they might have in store?"

She knew he was right. She had to monitor and keep a sharp watch. Nervous butterflies launched themselves in her queasy stomach. Just one more damn thing to worry about.

"Fine. Bring me something to drink. Water or a diet drink." She flashed him a confident look she didn't entirely feel, tucking the earbuds into place, prepared to listen in. She had a job to do.

An unexpected surge of heat energized her as she watched him walk down the street. She breathed in their tantalizing odor, still detectable in the closed confines of the truck's cab, sensing something huge, something life-changing was a foot. *Tonight.* Tonight, she'd get him alone. See if she could get him to open up more, tell her what she already knew, because that would be the beginning. Recognizing past hurts. And choosing to share. A truth slipped past her defenses as the world stilled for a moment. It wasn't only Cole that had been damaged by the past. She wasn't exactly forthcoming with him, either.

* * * *

What the fuck was I thinking? I have to slam a lid on this thing. Now. Before she gets hurt. Women always said they could handle a one-night stand, but he knew it to be a lie most of the time. They were nurturing, caring creatures — at least Gabby was, whether she wanted to recognize it or not. He pushed the difficult thoughts aside, finding that far harder than pushing open the café door. But it had to be done. He had to focus on the here and now.

A couple of patrons looked up as he entered, pretending indifference, as myriad cooking odors assailed his senses. The fragrance of Chinatown — rice, meat, oriental spices, soy and hot fat blended with sweet and sour, filling his nostrils with an explosion of anticipation. The customers sized him up silently, then looked away. It was a modest eatery, containing a few tables and a handful of black leatherette stools that had seen better days. He chose a stool from where he could see the rest of the room in the mirror behind the counter, spying Chang sitting with two men at a far table, his back protected by the wall behind him.

Cole had no time to notice more as the pretty dark-haired waitress with a perky ponytail picked up the coffeepot, the question plain on her face as she glanced his way, filling his ceramic white cup to the brim at his nod.

"Thanks," he said, adding a smile to his greeting, sneaking his hand under the chair's edge to plant one of the bugs at the same time he sat. *Time to go to work.* "What's a pretty girl like you doing in a dive like this? With a face like yours, you should be auditioning for the movies. I think there's enough production companies in Vancouver now you'd stand a great chance of getting a role."

"I don't have time to go to the movies, let alone audition for one. Besides, many pretty girls in Chinatown." She smiled, showing her pleasure, and handed him the laminated menu, plucking it out from between the sugar container and the paper napkin holder.

"Special is won ton soup and grilled cheese. It's homemade and very good," she said, enunciating the second language carefully.

"That eclectic pairing of Chinese and Canadian cuisine does sound good, but not nearly as good as you agreeing to go out on a date with me," he replied, giving her a speculative glance and tucking the menu back in place. It had left a sticky residue on his fingers.

"I'm not supposed to date customers," she whispered, her glance toward Chang telling the story.

"Sure you can't make an exception? I know this probably sounds made up, but I swear it's true — I have a good friend who's part of a production team for a movie company based right here in Vancouver. Perhaps I can introduce you to him? He says they're always looking for a fresh face. I'm certain once he sees you, he'll be as impressed as I am."

Bingo. The waitress's beautiful eyes lit up with speculation. "You do that for me, a stranger?"

"Well, I really do hope we won't remain strangers for too long, darlin'," he said, smiling with a hint of suggestion, adding a pure Texan drawl to his voice.

"I'm not sure." A frown creased her forehead as she hesitated.

"Could I have a glass of water while you think about how great it would be to go out to a fancy restaurant?

You can get all dolled up, have a free dinner, maybe get a small part in a movie. What's to think about? How about Sunday night? Surely, your boss gives you one day off a week?" he pressed.

"Maybe. Bottled or tap?"

"Bottled. Where's your restroom?"

She pointed to a narrow hallway that led into the back, right beside the kitchen. "First door."

"Thanks. See you soon, beautiful."

Cole pretended nonchalance as he got up. In the men's, he washed his hands after planting a bug under the sink. They didn't need video, just sound, as disgusting as even that was and he couldn't be sure that important conversations wouldn't happen in the men's bathroom. God, she was listening in to him hitting on the waitress. Well, fuck, she was a professional. She'd understand.

He exited the bathroom, careful not to touch anything and pick up another other kind of disgusting bug. The operation to plant the surveillance device went smoothly, no one taking notice of him as he slid back onto the stool. Chang was ignoring the clientele for the most part, busy writing with a mechanical pencil from time to time in a large black book that looked like an old-fashioned ledger with ruled lines, at a table as far from the entrance as he could manage in the small business. A pair of men sat across from him, their backs to Cole and the room. He would ask them something, they would answer quietly and Chang would jot something down. One of the young men had a distinctive bark of a laugh that grated on Cole's nerves each time he heard it. God, but Cole itched to take a look at that book Chang seemed so obsessed with.

Cole assessed the man while his waitress was busy. Middle-aged, slight with a small pot belly, a few streaks of gray marring the oiled hair combed back so smoothly to his skull that comb marks were apparent. It was clipped carefully over his ears. Graying whiskers covered his chin. His dark eyes flitted back and forth, from the what looked like Chinese businessmen he appeared to be giving the third-degree to and the book he wrote in, his expression cold and unyielding, not-so-subtle power obvious in every gesture he made.

He looked up all of a sudden, locking dark obsidian eyes with Cole. The dead-snake look of a killer. Chang assessed him with straight forward focus as he stared for longer than necessary at Cole. The man was telling him plain and simple that he was the one on foreign territory, Chang territory. Cole gave him back the goods, his ire at the man's exploits turning his expression cold and calculating. Oh, yeah, they had each other's measure all right. Good old-fashioned Mexican stand-off right there in the center of Chinatown.

"Food's ready." The waitress planted the soup with the sandwich nestled around it in front of Cole, giving him the perfect excuse to look away from the grim reality of the café's owner. She refilled his coffee cup, though he had only taken a couple of sips.

"Thanks, beautiful." He gave her another smile. "You gonna go out with me? Take a chance at a better life?" He hated himself at that moment for the false promise, knowing all too well the girl's probable lot in life.

"You are very welcome, sir. And yes, I think I would very much like to have dinner with you and your friend." The waitress was all smiles now, though she kept her back toward Chang as she spoke, murmuring her responses. "You want anything else?"

"No, this is fine." He was hungry, the aroma drifting up from the soup and sandwich making his mouth water. He polished the food off in a matter of minutes and drained the cup of coffee.

"We've got fresh blueberry pie, very good," the waitress said as she poured him a third cup of coffee.

"Sure, why not?" he answered, spying a couple of young gang members striding in the front door, easily recognizing them from the recent photos sent by Quinn. They joined Chang and the others, huddling around the table.

The young girl scurried over to Chang's table, bowing slightly and asking the two hoods what they wanted.

One of them reached out and slid his hand under the edge of her uniform, making Cole wince though the young girl did not give away any emotion in her expression, remaining stoic. Oh, yeah, she had to be paying off her debt to Chang. *What a price.* Life was so unfair, so hard on the young. Especially the females. Was Pearl also doing the same? He shook his head. *Fucking dog-eat-dog world.*

He sipped his coffee patiently, waiting for the waitress to bring him his pie. No rush. He wanted to drag this out. Chang did not intimidate him one iota.

"Sorry," she said as she opened the desert case on the counter and slid a piece of pie onto a plate with the help of a pie server. "You want ice cream?"

"No worries. And yes, a scoop of vanilla would be great."

"No hurry to get back to work?" she asked, plunking the pie in front of him. She spoke louder now, as if she had been instructed to.

"No, beautiful, not today. It's my day off."

"Where do you work?" He caught Chang paying attention to his answer as well, just as Cole expected. He had his head cocked to the side, his cold eyes warning the other men at his table to shut up.

"I work not far from here. Just started. You know Walmart? I work in their IT department." It was always a good ploy. Every Canadian city had at least one of the ubiquitous retail stores. Plus, they were open twenty-four hours a day, employees coming and going all the time.

"You have the accent," she commented, busy placing the pie back in the case. Every action she made was economical.

"Yeah, I know. I used to live in the United States."

"Why come here to Canada?" She seemed mystified.

"A woman," he said in a rueful tone. "But it's over now. All on my own, though I hope it doesn't stay that way for long."

She blushed a pretty shade of pink, looking at him with extra interest for just a split second before scurrying back to Chang's table as the owner held up a commanding finger, beckoning her.

He ate his pie slowly, savoring its deliciousness. It had just been baked.

He kept his focus on his food, pretending indifference to the seething dragon's activities in the back corner. When it looked like nothing else could be learned, he stood and asked for his check, handing over a fifty-dollar bill. More than enough to give the girl a generous tip.

She passed him his change, her back to Chang. A folded piece of paper nestled beside the golden-colored coins, and he tucked it in his pocket, knowing it would be her phone number. What a shit-heel. When this was over, he was going to do something for her and Pearl. Give them a chance at their dreams, call in favors, whatever it took.

He gave her a small salute of respect, touching his hand to his forehead, and exited the café.

* * * *

"Confucius say by three methods we learn wisdom. First, by refection, which is noblest. Second by imitation, which is easiest. And third, by experience, which is bitterest," Chang said, keeping his eye on the patrons as he repeated, with care, one of his favorite quotes from the master to the men watching him as if they had never heard it before. He didn't like the man at the counter talking to his waitress. He was trouble. Every male customer over eighteen looked like trouble to him, but this guy, he rubbed him far harder than most, giving him such a look in his own place. Customers. Always wanting to fuck his waitresses and not pay for the privilege. *You want fuckie-fuckie, go to Paradise and pay for it. Otherwise, leave women alone.*

The others waited for him to continue. Chang pulled at his chin whiskers, assessing. So much to consider, and as always, little time to prepare. He sighed, feeling the burden of decades of leadership, fighting for his clan and his people. The past twenty years business had been good, but like the *I Ching*, his bible for viewing the world, he had to consider the necessity of change. Was he falling out of touch? No, the old ways had always worked and would continue to work. Proof was in how well the Chang clan was doing, following the old path.

Let the young make mistakes, not see and learn from history. He was smarter than that.

"I will see you later." He dismissed the two businessmen keeping him up to date on all things happening in Chinatown. They bowed slightly and shuffled out.

Chang waited until they had cleared the doorway, glancing at his nephew.

"Have you done what I have asked?"

"Yes, Uncle. Supplies are out back, in my van. Ready to bring in."

"Good, good." Chang nodded. "Bring them in later, after the lunch rush leaves."

Tommy gave him a questioning look, then a quick glance over at Lee. "We heard something, something about the goods at the docks."

Chang grunted, his gaze shifting back and forth from his black book to the asshole at the counter. Still chatting up May Lin.

"Yeah, what about them?"

"A new customs agent has been asking questions down at the docks about our business. All in our business, like he not aware of the deal."

"What kind of questions?"

Tommy shrugged. "About what's in the packages. Stuff like that."

"What? What guy? What he look like?"

"I got a picture," Tommy said, handing over his burner phone that Chang had supplied.

Chang studied the photo, narrowing his eyes. "Hmm, don't know him. Anybody talk?"

"No—nothing," Tommy assured him, his eyes suggesting shock at the mere suggestion of anyone saying anything to someone outside their community.

"Good. Don't matter. Deliveries about to leave soon anyway. That take care of the problem." Chang cracked his face into what he thought of as a benevolent smile.

Finally, the guy he was watching left the café. He let out a frustrated sigh. "Okay, hurry up and unload supplies. No time to waste. Go out the back way."

The pair jumped to do his bidding. He nodded for more coffee and when the waitress reached out to pour him a refill, he reached out and grasped her wrist.

"What the guy want?"

"Nothing, sir. Very polite," May Lin said, managing to keep hold of the pot. She knew better than to drop it or even to ask who he meant.

"Sure, sure. Just polite. You be careful around guys like him. Nothing but trouble. Only want one thing."

She nodded, and waited for him to let go of her wrist. He did, but not before adding, "Never forget who I am. Who you owe everything to. You don't like this job, I can find you one at Paradise. Working with those girls."

She kept her eyes downcast as she poured his coffee. "I like it here. I never forget," she said, her tone subdued and respectful, her hand shaking.

He grunted. May Lin didn't have to worry. He had no intention of sending her down the street to the massage parlor. But it never hurt to make sure she knew the abyss she was stretched over. Time to pay Vu a visit. See if he knew the guy asking questions. He tucked Tommy's phone with the photo of the guy in his pocket and got up to walk the short distance that separated their businesses. Vu would know who he was if anyone did.

* * * *

Cole opened the truck door, making Gabby start. She had been listening in, multi-tasking with video from Quinn, aware Cole was on his way and wanting to pretend nonchalance. She flashed him a steely glance from under her lashes.

"All done?" she asked, patting herself on the back for her professionalism. He was just like all men, looking for a pretty woman to flirt with. *Probably going to swear it was all business, too, yeah, right, and if that was believable, I have a bridge to sell.*

"Yeah, got it done." He looked over at her, an old-soul smile coming over his face, lighting up his eyes. She watched it emerge, his entire face turning golden, making something quicken inside her. *Goddamn it! Why?* How could she sense so much about him just through eye contact alone? Well, that and some pretty fantastic sex. Were the legends true then? Or was it just heightened emotion due to the extreme circumstances they found themselves in? She realized belatedly she hadn't reacted to his comment and he was waiting. He spoke again, adding a comment tinged with satisfaction. "And there's no way they're going to find those bugs."

"What do you mean?"

"Before coming to Vancouver, I had just finished inventing a new kind of prototype listening device that mimics the frequency of any known bug sweeper, so the gang won't know they're there. The bugs, in essence, become invisible to the wand. At least for now, anyway. Technology always keeps up after a short lull, but right now, we've got the edge."

"Really? That is impressive." She noticed the blinking red light on the monitor. "Something's up. Quinn just called for a video conference."

She pushed a button on the console, and Quinn's face filled the screen. "Bad news, I'm afraid. The FBI and the RCMP are in the middle of running a sting operation. You know, like the takedown of the Hell's Angel in Winnipeg and the Rock Machine in Quebec a few years back. We can't expect any cooperation. In fact, they explicitly warned us to stay out of their way. That bigger things were at stake."

Cole gave a huge sigh. "Talk about bad timing."

Gabby's stomach tightened with fresh worry. Having the authorities on board would have been helpful.

She continued listening with one ear to the ongoing conversation in the café's men's room while multitasking with Cole and Quinn still discussing logistics.

"Hey, listen to this." Gabby unplugged her headphones, letting the voices she'd been monitoring enter the cab of the truck unimpeded.

"Uncle won't care. Come on, let's go and have some fun. We've earned it, bro! We can finish this shit up later." The sounds of water running muffled another voice. Then the hot air dryer blasted out, making it impossible to hear for a few seconds.

"No time today. Maybe tomorrow."

"Shit, why wait? What if she's gone by then?"

"Who pays you? You want to move up in this organization — you work first. Besides, the ship doesn't sail until Monday." The guy gave a snort of derision.

Cole sat as if electrified as the voices moved away and the noise of the bathroom door closing came over the airwaves. "They sound like the two mutts sitting with Chang earlier. Christ, I wonder if they're talking about Sara? We've got to tail them if they leave here. Did you hear that, Quinn? I'm calling Jake. She must be at the docks." Excitement lined Cole's tone as he punched in Jake's number.

Gabby couldn't believe their luck. It all made sense now. "I'll bet it's a cargo ship. And that must mean she's in a shipping container!" Her heart hammered, making it difficult to breathe. It was a natural — many people had been smuggled out from China in the dangerous conditions of a cargo hold. Some made it out alive, some did not. Only, this time, a reverse trip was in the making. Every instinct in her body screamed it to be the answer.

"I'm calling this in." Cole's expression tightened as he conveyed the gist of the conversation from the bathroom of Chang's Café over the phone to Quinn. "Yeah, we're on it. We need to know for certain and we need to check vehicle registrations. Can you take care of it?"

A short pause. "Good." The call ended and Cole tucked the phone away.

"Quinn's on top of it." He started the truck. "Let's drive around and see if we can spot anything in the back lane. Maybe you can put a hat on, so they don't remember you from earlier."

She reached into the back seat and grabbed a baseball cap with the logo from the LA Kings hockey team blazoned on the crest. "*Really?*" she teased as she pulled the gray and black hat down tightly onto the crown of her head, tugging her hair through the loop in the back.

"Guess I'll need a new one now that I'm in Canuck-land."

She swatted at his arm, good spirits restored with the break in the case. "You're so bad."

"I'm so bad, I'm good," he quipped back.

Hmm. "That you are." She arched an eyebrow at him. She swallowed hard at his wolfish grin. *Good to be alive today.*

As Cole cranked the wheel hard and merged again with the busy traffic on Pender Street, she swung her head back and forth to catch everything. The back lane was barely wide enough to thread the vehicle through and he drove around obstacle after obstacle. Right behind Chang's business, a black van stood parked. Its back doors were flung open but the vehicle was tight against the building, making it impossible to see what was inside.

As Cole moved at a snail's pace, Gabby made a quick decision. "I'm checking it out." And before he could object, she hit the Unlock button on the door and jumped down to the pavement. She pulled the brim of her hat lower then, at a fast clip, raced to the van, grinning at Cole's horrified expression. He didn't know who she was if he thought she'd leave one stone unturned. One never knew what slime-bucket would crawl out.

The van windows were tinted, but with her hands acting like binders braced on both sides of her face, she could see inside enough to make out some boxes. And what was inside made her heart slam. Boxes of nails and liter-sized Mason jars. Worst of all, a small box of what looked like dynamite.

"Hey, what you doing? Get away from there," a loud voice ordered. She spun around, face-to-face with one of the men from Quinn's collection of photos. He'd come out the man door beside the van. His hardened expression turned her stomach.

"Sorry, just looking," she said, pretending to be indifferent to whatever was inside, keeping her head down.

"Whatcha think this is? Nothing here for you." The angry young man looked to be still in his teens, his scraggly chin whiskers adding a pathetic belligerence to his pinched face.

She moved away, not wanting any sudden movement to set him off.

"You have any change you can spare?" she asked, trying to sound desperate.

"I don't help out junkies. Unless you want to earn it?" he said, his eyebrows shooting upward with the off-color suggestion. *Yuck.*

"I'm no fuckin' prostitute!" She didn't have to pretend she was insulted.

"Hey, Tommy, what's up?" Another teenager had emerged from the building.

Two against one. She turned and hurried away, praying they weren't going to give chase. But, if they did, she knew a lot of solid moves, thanks to Combato and Defendo, programs developed by ex-military Bill Underwood for the Canadian Military and the martial arts scene after WW II, but why engage unless there was no other choice?

Any second she expected to feel a slimy hand on her shoulder, making her body crawl with worry as she strode away, pretending indifference. When she was far enough away that she knew they hadn't bothered with her but were continuing about their business, she offered up a prayer. *Thank you, God.*

She found Cole parked in his truck a couple of hundred feet away just around the corner and out of sight of the van, his expression suggesting he was not entirely pleased with her. She climbed inside. He attacked before she could get a word in.

"What the hell, Gabby, you could have been hurt!" He stared at her, his angry, very worried eyes drilling into her soul and pining her to the seat with their sheer intensity. "I can't have you going off half-cocked like that! For God's sake, woman, we need to keep on the same page, plan our moves! Oh, God, if you had been hurt, I— I won't allow it!"

His words lit a firestorm.

"For fuck's sake, Cole, what was I supposed to do? It was the ideal opportunity! And you are not my father, like I'm not your mother! About as far from that as two people can be! I'm perfectly capable of taking care of myself. I'm a professional, not a fucking amateur, not a bimbo like that woman in the massage parlor or that oh-so-sweet one in the café. I don't trade favors. I bed you, it's because I want to. Not because I'm trading something for it."

Complete silence filled the cab.

Gabby took a few breaths, her heart racing far too fast, her thoughts in turmoil. Danger lurked at every corner, and the one to her heart looked to be the one most likely to trip her up.

"Okay, I'm sorry. I was out of line."

"Do you think?" She rubbed at her forehead as she snapped out her answer. "Okay, I know you've been hurt, Cole, lost people, but I'm a strong, resilient person. I don't give up when the going gets rough. I hang in there, have no doubt on that score. I'm in this for the long haul. Whatever it takes, I'll be there."

She took a chance and looked at him. Indecision carved sharp lines into his skin, bruising the skin under his eyes with dark shadows.

"And I found out something very important. They're planning on making incendiary devices. The van's loaded with Mason jars, hundreds of small nails and sticks of dynamite."

Cole let out a long breath as he assessed her information, drumming his fingers on the steering wheel, his jaw tightly clenched. "Looks like Chinatown's headed for a protracted war. I have no damn choice. This will have to be reported through proper channels whether we like it or not. God, I hope we can contain this. Last thing we need is to have Chang know we're this close." He took another breath, shaking his head. "As if this city doesn't have enough trouble already with the current opioid crisis."

"You know about that?" Though it was hard to miss, ambulances, triage staging areas, paramedics and firefighters attending to someone else lying prone on the streets.

"Who doesn't? Hundreds of overdoses every month—it's beyond comprehensible. How the fuck do we stop them? Get them to quit before they throw their lives away?" His pain-riddled eyes bruised her soul.

"You can't blame yourself for choices that other people make, Cole. You can only be there when they are ready to accept help."

He slammed his fist into the steering wheel, making her wince. That had to hurt.

"Sorry, I snapped." His eyes swam with emotion, a rueful grin melting her right to the core when he looked up and locked glances with her.

"You did nothing wrong." She hesitated. "If you want to talk about it, like I said, I'm a good listener." She held her breath. *Please. Let some of the pain out. For God's sake.*

Silence descended. She supposed the moment lost. *Fine.* She'd given him the chance.

But then he began to speak, almost as if he were talking to himself, words pouring out in a raging torrent. "Mathew, my son, he was a special little guy. Bright as a whip and so curious about life. It was so hard to keep him out of anything, to keep him safe. The day it happened —" He darted a quick glance her way, his expression laced with pain so harsh she could barely stand seeing it. "Mathew had been running around while his mother sat on the park bench, talking with other mothers of the play group she belonged to. She wasn't watching closely, just nodding at his exploits. Just a normal day in paradise."

He ran his hand over his head, then tightened it on the back of his neck in a stranglehold.

"A monster was watching from the bushes, waiting for his chance. He had a van parked on the street a short distance away, a rag soaked with chloroform in his hands. We found the evidence. He threw it onto the ground. He managed to get to the van, though Mathew put up a hell of a fight. One of his little sports shoes came off..." Cole voice trailed off and he pressed his lips tightly together. His hands moved to the steering wheel, clutched at it as if it were a lifeline, his knuckles white from the strain.

He turned the eyes of pain and death onto Gabby. She sat stock-still, unable to move or speak.

"Then, things just fell apart. Maddie began using, couldn't handle losing her little boy. I failed them. There are things you can never un-see. I should have been there..."

Tears escaped. He dashed them away with an angry hand. "I'm sorry. I'm damaged goods, Gabby. I have nothing to give you or any other woman. Only good to be the avenger of death."

"For fuck's sake, *no*! You are so much more than that, Cole. You have to forgive yourself for this. It was not your fault. Evil exists in this world. Hell, it's a daily fight for some to keep it at bay. Good people are hurt by others every minute of every day. Why should any of us think we're so special that we should be spared? What, so someone else undergoes it instead? Is that right? No, it happens. Shit happens. But at least you picked yourself up, got back to work, and channeling all that pain to help others. Trust that this is your path — avenging evil in this world. I know. A man harmed me. Left me at the mercy of a loan shark. I could have fallen into the pit. But no, I'm using that hard-earned experience to help women who need out of bad situations. Who need proof to keep their children safe. To move on and rebuild their lives." Gabby threw out all the lifelines she could, hoping one would be the one to spare him.

Silence.

Cole stared ahead, his eyes narrowed.

"Someone tried to hurt you?" he asked, turning toward her, locking eyes with her. She broke the connection first.

"It's a long story. But my ex was a gambler and got into debt so badly that he fled the country with his tail between his legs. I was left to pay them off, or lose a limb, and I am kind of partial to all of mine." She heard the shakiness in her tone. Couldn't be helped. The last few minutes had blown her away.

"I am sorry. Your life hasn't been easy, either."

"No one has it easy. My grandma always said, 'it's damn hard to be human, child, but it's all we got'."

"No kidding." Though still shaken, Cole sounded better.

"Okay," he said, straightening his shoulders. He pulled out a laptop and connected to the satellite system, bringing up the Department of Motor Vehicles, hacking in within a few seconds. She understood. She'd break a few more rules, if it would bring Sara home sooner.

He turned to Gabby, all business now, his eyes clearer. "The van's registered to Core Enterprises. Hmm, that's a new one."

"Let me check on it," Gabby said, itching to get to the truth. *Is it a Chang company or not?*

Cole gave her some room to work as his cell phone rang.

"Aha, here we go!" she said with satisfaction, finding the exact information they needed a few minutes later. "Chang *is* one of the partners."

"Good work. Okay, we'll follow it if it leaves the area. And Silk just called to say they've scheduled two teams of low-level TETRAD operatives to relieve us in a couple of hours, then we grab a few hours of sleep. I don't expect the two pervs will head to the docks until tomorrow at the earliest, but you never know, what with the threat of gang warfare hanging over everyone's head."

She began to voice her objections. "I can work all night, sleep right here—"

"No, you need your rest. Too many mistakes are caused by over-worked, sleep-deprived agents.

Cole started up the truck. "I'll reposition." He drove down the street, parking so they had a view of the area behind Chang's Café, and cut the motor.

"They just might lead us right to Sara." Gabby nodded as she spoke, keeping the peak of her hat low as she peered out her side window.

"We can only hope. And maybe offer up a prayer."

"You believe in God, Cole?" She surprised herself in the asking, but the isolation of the cab invited confessions. Stake-outs were notorious for this. They were also notorious for long hours punctuated by extreme need for action. A crazy life for sure, but one she wouldn't give up for anything. And when they solved the case or got the culprit or found someone and reunited them with their loved ones, it more than made up everything.

"I did. Not so sure these past few years. How about you?"

"I'd like to think someone is in charge of all this chaos. And the world is a remarkable place. Miracles happen every day in nature. And I was baptized Catholic as a child."

He shrugged as he reconnected to Quinn. "We need a miracle, so any help we can get is more than welcomed."

Gabby chewed on a fingernail as she monitored the noises and conversations in the café, kept an eye on her surroundings and listened in to Cole report her recent findings.

"Okay, good, here's what I suggest. Have someone call in an anonymous tip on an untraceable line. Then Chang will be none the wiser. Good, catch you later." Cole disconnected the call.

"That'll work." She nodded. "Good thinking. And to think I was just about ready to grab a cab to the police station and try to come up with a story on the way to explain seeing those bombs."

"No cab. I would have driven you there. And any excuse you came up with would have been lame, anyway. No way to explain our being here."

She sat back, stymied. "You're a kind of a control freak," she grumbled, letting off some steam as she cooled her heels. Any banter was welcome after the past few minutes.

He shrugged. "I was raised this way. Blame my southern mama."

"I don't think stakeouts are the kind of situation that have proper southern protocols attached."

"Are you kidding me? I've been instructed exactly how to act in any given situation."

"Say what?" The slight curve upward of his mouth said he was teasing her. The moment of brevity after the revelation took her breath clear away. If they could get this shit behind them, perhaps there was some hope for them.

"There they are. The two guys to watch the front entrance. A second pair of agents to take over for us will be here soon as well. Then, we can take a break." Cole sat up straighter. Gabby watched a pair of operatives she knew slightly drive by in a black SUV on their way to setting up their own stakeout in the front of Chang's.

"You should spend some time with your brother while he's here in town." The sudden thought was out of her mouth before she could stop it, not realizing it had been lurking in the back of her mind since she'd found out he called.

"And you should keep thoughts like that to yourself," he snapped back, stunning her. His brother was one sore point. The guy was as far from being easy as one could get.

"Fine. Be that way." She crossed her arms over her chest, pissed.

"I'm sorry. That was harsh."

"Do ya think?" She kept her eyes focused on the landscape, avoiding showing him the pain she'd experienced at his rebuttal. She already felt out of sorts arguing over the van incident. And what if Sara had been inside? A long shot, but not out of the question.

"I really am sorry, beautiful. Been a hell of a year."

She softened a bit. *Nice to be called beautiful, apology aside.* "Yeah, I get it. Just forget it happened. I've had far harsher words thrown my way from far lesser men."

"That doesn't make it right. You deserve so much better."

"What do you know about what I deserve?" she asked, making light of it. There would likely be a lot more hours with them holed up together and the last thing she wanted was to be at loggerheads the entire time.

This time, she met his glance, and when her eyes locked with his, that overwhelming sense of connection made her swallow hard. *Damn, alive and searing.* The knowledge burned within her. They needed time away from the job or the lust that was threatening to burst into flames around them would combust again. Of that she had no doubt.

She reached out on impulse, covering the back of his hand resting, unclenched at the moment, on the steering wheel.

"How about we make a pact. No harm intended."

"For real?" She watched his eyes open wider with surprise. His other hand came down over the top of hers, trapping it against the wheel, sending her senses reeling. "I'd like that. Never trusted a woman to have my back before."

"Never?" Gabby was shocked. "Not even when you took your wedding vows?"

His eyes closed. He pulled his hands away and didn't supply an answer.

Way to go, Gabby. Why don't you just dig it all up again. She must be shakier than she realized, not keeping a lid on that for now.

"Cole—"

"Gabrielle, please. Let's just keep our minds focused on business. Okay?" His expression tightened.

"Sure, I'm sorry." She pretended to pull a zipper across her mouth, hoping to draw a smile, reclaim that moment of brevity from earlier. Not to be. He took up a small white bud and pressed it into place in his ear canal, not looking her way.

Damn, at this rate, I'll never get to fully scratch this annoying itch. And it was annoying her, beyond all reason that she wanted to fuck Cole again, especially after his having opened up to her, trusted her, and now she couldn't control her raging hormones. They just needed to go to bed again and that would solve the problem, right?

She pressed the heel of her hand to her head. A tension headache loomed.

"You okay?" Cole asked.

"Yeah, fine."

Her phone buzzed, interrupting. *Celine.*

"Hey, what's up?" Gabby asked, focused on the steady stream of passersby, glancing over at the alleyway. So far, no one had exited the back of Chang's and the van remained parked.

"Just checking in. How's it going?"

"Peachy."

"That bad, eh? Just wanted to be sure you're okay. Can I bring you anything? I'm in the area."

"No, I'm fine. Best to stay away."

"Talkative today, aren't we?" Her sister knew her too well.

"Yeah, well, trying to make lemonade here." She closed her eyes for a second, the throbbing in her temples increasing.

Celine snorted. "Good luck with that. Text me if you need anything."

"Thanks."

Cole looked over at her, but made no comment as she ended the call. Her nerves were frayed from the stress. A new partner with so much baggage was daunting. But to also be ridiculously attracted wasn't helping one iota. And she had to keep it together. For Sara's sake. *Please, just let this case be blown wide open*, she prayed, *and we bring her home. Soon.*

Chapter Six

Cole tried in vain to keep his mind off having Gabby so close in the confines of the truck, giving off a fragrance that would test the restraint of a saint. Opening up to her had reduced his stress, made him feel closer to her. Something he had to be careful of. He was no good for her. Instead, he tried to focus on the wisdom of Sun Tzu's *The Art of War*, and the importance of foreknowledge, that the gaining of it through the five types of spies, no matter the cost, was essential. And if it carried with it the hope of carrying false tidings to the enemy, so much the better. Keeping Chang in the dark was their best chance of getting Sara back. Being where they weren't expected. And once they knew her exact location, he'd set the rest of his plan in action. As always, he tried to foresee every eventuality, every possible scenario ahead of time, and prepare in the hopes that one of the routes would lead to success.

The cops had come and gone with nothing changing, even after a careful search of the van.

He glanced over at Gabby from time to time as they waited, suspended in time. The heightened sense of continual readiness was beginning to take its toll on Gabby—that was obvious by the drooping of her eyelids as she rubbed at them furiously.

"Hey, beautiful, how you doing?" he asked. It was long past the time they could have left for the night, but she had insisted on staying there, not wanting to miss anything.

She licked her lips and his eyes followed the action. Fucking hard, so close and yet so far. He couldn't from staring at their deep pink plushness. It was everything he could do not to jump on top of her right there and fuck everything else going on. Could fate have landed him in a more difficult situation? Someone must be laughing their ass off at his expense right now somewhere in the vast universe.

Unbearable. He took a breath, forcing the image of Gabby naked and underneath him out of his brain. She had been so willing earlier, so wet and giving of herself. God, to be inside her once more would be worth any risk.

"I'm okay. We could sleep in shifts. Stay the night," she said, yawning to make her point.

"No, we're calling it a night. The second team has arrived. They don't need us to stay. You need to refresh yourself, sleep. Take a shower, eat, do whatever you require."

"Okay."

Cole breathed a sigh of relief and sped away from the curb. He pulled up in front of her townhouse a short while later.

"Want to come up? Have a drink?" she asked, without looking at him. She was fidgeting in her seat as she asked, her eyes focused somewhere else. Then she turned those baby blues eyes on him and gave him a smoldering glance from underneath thick lashes.

He should say no, keep her at arm's length. But instead other words formed and dropped from his mouth as if it had disconnected from his brain and reconnected with a more vital area — his cock. "A drink sounds good."

* * * *

Chang pursed his thin lips and narrowed his coal-black eyes in thought when the two brazen police officers strode right through his front door, right into the middle of a special clan supper, too. He ran his hand over his shiny black hair, making sure it was still in place. He tugged at his whiskers, wondering if he should try to darken them or shave, now that his beard was threaded with gray. He glanced back at the men who were looking around with curiosity clear in their expressions, there for some annoying purpose. *Have these men no honor?* He gave a sideways glance at Tommy, signaled with a finger to his nose. He watched his nephew scurry away while he kept the cops in his peripheral vision as he always did with all who entered his domicile, waiting for them to make the first move. Did this have something to do with what had happened earlier? The guy asking about their business interests at the docks? It was not often law enforcement crossed his doorstep and he would prefer it stayed that way.

He held his first grandchild on his lap, feeding her bits of sweet rice cake, enjoying how her golden-brown fawn-like eyes followed his every move as he fed her the honey-laced treat from his fingertips. He ignored the small looks of chagrin his wife, Missy Lin Flowers, kept directing his way, regarding him as the usurper of motherly authority. The mother didn't want her daughter, Jennifer, fed anything made from honey. *Most natural thing in the world, bees make it, full of minerals and vitamins, good for a child.* Bah, if not seeing that, some women were too quick to leave the ancient ways behind. *Should have the guidance of an arranged marriage like his parents did for him. None of this falling in love first. You fall in love later, after a proper partner is chosen.* What was good for generations of Changs was still good enough.

The two blue-uniformed men wormed their way through the Chang clan packing the restaurant, the jangling of the officers' handcuffs, radios, guns, batons and flashlight on their black leather belts heard even above the riotous laughter and conversations of so many relatives. The Chang clan was growing each year as more marriages and babies came along, a fact Chang was very proud of. As usual, he commanded from the back table pushed against the wall so no one could creep up on him unnoticed. *Best place to oversee operations.* He handed the toddler over to her mother as the men stopped in front of him. All three of them watched the red-gowned woman with the white orchid pinned to the bodice sweep her daughter away to a far table, fussing over the child, wiping the sticky grains of rice away from her rosebud lips.

"Beautiful child," one office said with a nod at Jennifer, not so happy on her mother's lap as she began to fuss about, wanting more treats. Her little fingers clutched at thin air, signaling her need.

"Yes, what can I do for you, officers?" Chang asked with careful politeness, gesturing for them to sit. No point in making new enemies. He now had plenty of room at the table as family members melted away.

"You are registered as the owner of the van out back. We need to see your license and registration. Would you mind getting those things and accompanying us outside?"

"Would you care for refreshments first? Food? Drink?" he asked. He prayed Tommy had managed to finish the unloading, hiding the explosives where they could not be found, not by an outsider who did not know Chinatown's underground network.

"No, we've fine. We're here on official business. There's been an anonymous tip that we need to investigate."

"Officers, are you familiar with the wisdom of Confucius?" he asked, walking the two men through the back of the café and into the alley behind. The van was parked with its back end up against the building and he stopped in front of it, turning around to watch their reactions.

"Confucius? He was Chinese, right?" one asked, scratching the back of his neck with a big meaty paw of a hand. Both men dwarfed Chang, towering over him, the blue mantle of authority leeching out of every pore.

"Yes, Chinese, most correct. He was a very wise man of vision. Lived long time ago. 'If you see what is right and fail to act on it, you lack courage'. You men, you practice and honor his teachings every day, going out into the world with the courage to act on what you know to be right. Very honorable."

Chang patted himself on the back for coming up with the right compliment for the occasion. Confucius had words of wisdom for all people, all the time. He narrowed his eyes, picturing his nephew, unhappy with something he'd seen in Tommy's eyes a few times of late when Tommy had thought he wasn't being observed. Boy had too much ambition for one so young. *May need his wings clipped, learn new respect for his elders. Maybe Vu was right? Nephew not respecting the old ways.*

"Well, good, we do what we can to serve the people. Now, if you would just show us your papers?"

"Yes, yes, I have my license right here. Papers are in the glove box." Chang pulled out his black leather wallet and slid out his license. He handed it over. The man checked it, pursing his lips as he read the pertinent details. Chang knew what it contained. Photo ID of a man of average height and weight, but what was not listed was his unusually high IQ of 147. Too bad. Very impressive number. The other officer strode by him and up to the panel side window, using his hands cupped to his face to allow him to peer inside. Chang watched him, listening to his boots crunch on the gravel of the parking lot. *A noisy man, never catch anyone unaware like that.*

"Who drives the van? Anyone other than you?" the other officer who took his license asked, checking the date stamp on it to see if it was still valid. It was. One thing Chang knew, don't give them a reason to pull him over. More than one idiot had been taken down and had numerous offenses added on for drug possession, etc., just because of a broken tail light or an outdated license. *Stupid fools.* Not catch him like that. Did no one think to watch that new television show, *Live PD*, showing how stupid most criminals were? No wonder cops caught them. Chang felt nothing but contempt for such imbecile behavior. Deserved to get caught.

"Many drivers. All employees have access to it, to haul supplies for the business."

"You have the keys on you?"

Chang pulled the extra key fob from his black dress pants pocket and pressed the unlock mechanism. He went to open the glove box himself.

"No, I'll do that. Step aside," the police officer said, waving him away.

His breathing sped up, though he would allow none of it to show, just waited for the cop to check it out. Was the gun gone as instructed? Nephew would be in deep shit if not. Have wings clipped for certain.

"Well, it all seems in order," the lawman said after giving the papers a thorough check and calling the number in over his radio attached to his shoulder, checking with dispatch if the van number matched with the registration. "Mind if we look inside?" If they were asking, then they had not spotted evidence so far. If they had, he'd be in cuffs and they would be searching his pockets. Chang took a satisfied breath. Tommy had finished in time.

"No problem, go right ahead. Chang always stay on right side of law," he said with a grand sweeping gesture of his arm. The officers just grunted and got down to work. Inspecting every square inch of the van, but coming up empty. So sad. Chang hid a satisfied smile, mentally thanking Vu for the heads up. Now he had bigger fish to fry as he turned his mind to the latest intel. Things were getting heated in Chinatown, enemies closing in all direction. Time for Chang to send his own message.

* * * *

Day Four: 1:13 a.m.

What am I doing? This is not going to stop at one drink. But the words had come unheeded from her mouth and she could not take them back. Hell, truth be told, she wanted this to happen again. Wanted to forget everything for a precious bit of time. Loose herself in the moment. She was too discombobulated with lust from having to sit by Cole for hours on end, body twitching with desire. *Well, at least between the over-the-top action parts of the day. Just a couple of uninterrupted hours – that's all I ask. Maybe then I can get this incessant lust to go away. Focus just on the job.*

"What's your poison?" she asked, unlocking the front door.

"Uh, anything really." He cleared his throat, his warm brown eyes locking glances with her, smoldering passion obvious in the dark depths.

"I got it all thanks to all the parties lately. Celine just loves to entertain. Every kind of alcohol —"

He interrupted. "Yeah, you got it all, beautiful. The whole package. Everything a man could possibly want." What was there to say to that? She remembered to pull the door closed behind them. Her body began trembling at the sudden realization they were locking out the world, if only for a short while, making even that simple action difficult. His eyes became more intense as their gaze met again, the smoldering in their depths leaving her breathless. He towered above her, their height differences more obvious this close. *Too close.* And he smelled too good as she took a steadying breath, flooding her body with his scent.

He reached down and tucked a strand of hair behind her ear, the action tender, the look in his eyes so hungry she swallowed. Hard. Was she locking in the big bad wolf? The one who would eat her alive? She drew a shaky breath. Then she was lost as he pulled her into his arms, claiming her. His kiss. Nothing about it gentle and soft. But so much more. She was more than willing, letting him push his way inside her mouth. His tongue was warm as it twined with hers, stroked hers. Tantalized. Made her flood with wetness.

His big capable hands all over her were not nearly enough. She needed him elsewhere, everywhere. Right this instant. Fire erupted, charging every cell, every muscle with excitement. With lust. Heat poured onto the surface of her skin, driven by the blood coursing through her. She felt flushed and awestruck by the dizzying sensation, her knees turning to rubber.

She slid her hands down the solid powerful muscles of his back, feeling the smoothness and warmth of his skin as he pressed into her, claiming her mouth, her neck, her breasts as he jerked her top up, exposing her white lace bra.

Heat unfurled between her legs, inside the walls of her pussy the throbbing accelerated. Became frantic. She breathed in the scent of their mutual arousal, the length and breadth of his cock against her thigh mesmerizing, its immense size making her shaky as it pressed heavily. *I want him inside me. Now.*

The ache grew. He grasped one nipple with his lips, then the other, sucking on them hard right through the thin lace. Intense clenching pulsed rhythmically in her belly, firing off hot thrills to chase through her blood, scalding her even more. She was about to come. The sensation made her gasp aloud, and he stopped for a moment. *No. Don't stop.*

"We shouldn't be doing this. I can't offer you anything. I'm no good for you. No good for any woman."

"No, that's not true. I want this. I want you. Right now, Cole, that's all that matters. And who says it has to be anything more than what we want right now, right this minute? We're both past the age of consent." She was breathless with need, desperate to convince him to continue, her mind racing at the thought of not having this man, right here, right now.

She looked up and caught the indecision in his eyes. She reached for his hand. "Come, I'm taking you to bed. If we don't do something about this lust, so help me God, I'm going to go crazy here. Earlier, at the cemetery, that was just a quickie to keep us from exploding — you know, scratch the itch. I want everything now. I want to experience all of you."

He tightened his fingers around hers. "I want that too." His voice shook, endearing him to her even further as she led him from the room, down the hall and into her bedroom.

Not even bothering to pull back the covers, she tossed her phone onto the night stand and pulled him toward her, pressed herself tight up against him, wanting to be with him more than she had ever imagined possible. Like she always thought it should be. A desire to be with a man beyond all reason. Beyond all doubt. Like Tristan and Iseult had drunk from the cup of love. For her, it had to be overwhelming — if it was right.

As if in a trance, she pulled away and stripped the damp clothes from her overheated body, watching as he did the same. A warrior's body emerged, heavy muscles corded under a golden tan, a huge cock proud and ready. The dreamlike state continued as he pressed up against her, his need for her as obvious as her need for him. His mouth on hers. His hands on her body, so tight his fingers pressed into her flesh almost painful. He ravaged her mouth, scalding, tasting of blood and salt and fear.

Liquid flame engulfed her. She wound her arms around his neck, arched her body seeking his. His tugged on her nipples with his fingers, then his mouth as he sucked each one between his lips and into the heat, until she was twisting in agony.

"Fuck me, fuck me, now."

"You're killing me, beautiful. I need protection." It took a moment for understanding to dawn. What did he need protection from?

"Uh, in the night stand." He opened the top drawer and grabbed the small box, shaking out a silver-wrapped package. He tore it open with his teeth and rolled it down over his cock. She lay back on the bed and spread her legs for him, enjoying the lust that darkened his eyes even further, their shine visible under the glow of the night light.

He came to her then, his massive body looming over hers as he ran his hands all over her until she was trembling with pent-up passion. Caressing, tugging, kissing. treasuring her flesh as he nibbled his way down her body, not missing anything. She thrashed her head back and forth on the pillow, her desire to be possessed and loved overcoming any thought of shying away.

She came right off the bed as he ran a finger down her pussy, spreading the quivering lips. Every nerve ending alive, her blood sang with the thrill. He pushed a finger deep inside her channel, into the center of her heat, sending more pleasure zinging through her body. His warmth breath teased the sensitive tissues, dancing across her swollen clit and turning her to liquid flame. Every part of her was wide awake, searching, hungry, seething with unbridled lust, the pressure almost too much to bear.

"Please, please, fuck me," she said, her voice so low and throaty she barely recognized it.

"Not till I taste you, beautiful."

His words electrified the very air she was breathing.

He pressed his mouth against the juncture of her thighs, hot breath searing, velvet tongue lapping. She let loose wild moans, her small body too full of anticipation to keep it all inside. When she could handle no more, she mewed her surrender, driven nearly insane.

"Please, Cole," she whispered, so needy she could not imagine existing one more second without release from the unbearable pressure.

He moved, seeming to understand her desperateness. Centered himself between her shaking thighs and entered her in one amazing thrust, sending her senses reeling and reaching for climax.

"Oh, sweet heaven above," she moaned, hands firmly planted on his ass, forcing him to push into her as far as possible. Wonderful thrusts of intensive pure pleasure over and over until they became one bucking beast. One connected energy. And went over the top of the mountain together.

Her phone rang, jarring her from the afterglow of the best sex of her life. Wiping the stinging perspiration from her eyes, she fumbled to answer it.

"Hey, Silk," she said, trying in vain to sound normal while breathless, her heart hammering. Had it been that good between them? They might not see eye-to-eye on other issues, but right here — right now — in this bed, they saw things the same. And yes, if she had any say, there would be lots of this kind of action. *Oh no, I'd been thinking one tryst would solve my giant inch. So much for that idea.* Cole completed her. Made her feel things she had only imagined possible. And she was beyond certain at this moment he needed her just as much.

"What's up? You sound out of breath."

"Just raced for the phone. I was in the shower. What's the deal?"

"I'm checking in to let you know Chang's crew is on the move in the van. We've got a team following them right now."

"Where are they headed?"

"Not the docks, if that's what you were thinking. Okay, they just pulled up in front of an old apartment block. We'll keep you keep you posted if anything happens. Could you check on who owns it?"

"Sure."

She scrambled for a piece of paper and scribbled down the address of the building.

"Catch you later."

She looked over at Cole who had sat up, preparing to leave the bed. He tossed the used condom in the wastebasket, still turned away from her.

"You want to shower together?" she asked, running her hands down his back and experiencing the thrill at all that glorious undulating man muscle. "We got a couple more hours. Maybe take a nap after?"

"I've got to get going. Time's wasting," he said in an abrupt way, standing up, shaking her hand off.

"You still need to get cleaned up," she shot back, trying to hide her disappointment. "There's fresh towels in the cupboard under the sink."

He grunted and strode away, giving her a perfect view of his tight ass. And his obvious desire to get away as soon as possible.

A few seconds later, she heard the water running.

She sat there, fuming for a few seconds. *Benefit of the doubt, Gabby.* She recalled her words of earlier about meaning no harm. *Yeah, easier said than done.* She got up and pulled her robe on then walked into the tiny kitchen and made a pot of strong coffee. When it finished percolating through the machine, she filled a thermos with the hot brew.

A few minutes later, she heard his bootsteps echoing on the hardwood floors of the hallway before he emerged near the front door visible from the kitchen. He looked so damn good, fresh from the shower, his hair still damp. But his tight expression said it all. Closed for business. So much for all her good intentions.

"Here. Take this." She thrust the coffee at him, almost hitting him in his broad chest.

"Uh, Gabby, I'm sorry, for what it's worth. I told you I'm no good for you."

"Fine. Whatever." *Never trust a man. I should know better.* Just when she'd let herself think there might be some hope, damn it, he pulled away as though she was some kind of nuclear device.

"Don't be that way."

"What way is that, Cole, the same as you? Pretending this" — she pointed at him, then herself — "wasn't the best sex of your life? That there's no instant connection going on that defies all reason? Because I can do that, too. Shut this down, whatever *this* is." She crossed her arms over her chest and pressed her lips together, fighting tears. She was promising something she knew was impossible, but he didn't need to know that. And right now, no matter what the cost, she was no crybaby.

He looked as if he was going to say something more, then just shook his head and walked to the door. He turned back.

"I'll catch up with you at TETRAD. I've got some tech work to do. And, Gabby, for what it's worth, I don't mean you any harm. I want you to be happy and that's just not possible with the likes of me."

She bit her lip, unsure of herself, and not knowing the words that would convince him to stay. An impossible situation. They had no choice but to be in each other's company for who knew how long. It was going to be fucking torture, no doubt about it. She sighed, holding back the tears, and hurried off to shower. *Keep your mind on the job. Nothing else matters.*

* * * *

Day Four: 2:35 a.m.

What the hell was I thinking? I'm broken. It's far too late for me to even think I'm capable of being with another woman. I'm the worst person possible in the world for her. But even as he thought it, a small frisson of hope sparked and an ember came to life inside his soul. The missing part he was achingly aware of every moment of every day, the deep wide wound impossible to bear, began to close, defying all odds. But it was too unsettling. He tamped all such thoughts back down, headed to his truck. He had made his decision and now he must abide by it. *Keep Gabby safe.*

He drove to TETRAD, needing to be submerged in work. He found the office empty, thank God. Last thing he wanted was a discussion with anyone about anything other than getting Sara home.

Concentrating on discovering the owner of the apartment block Chang's van had parked at and channeling through a labyrinthine smokescreen that hid the true owner, he didn't hear the footsteps until it was too late.

He shut down the screen, spun around in his chair. "What the hell are you doing here?" He recognized the men. Chang and the two young men from the café. The unsmiling trio had him at a disadvantage. And he didn't fucking like it.

"It's time we became acquainted. You and your friends have been snooping around Chinatown and asking about me and my business interests. You should have come to me, no one else. Only I can set the record straight. Confucius very clear on this point. 'Before you embark on a journey of revenge, dig two graves'," Chang said, his sidekicks silent bookends, their appearance similar in the black clothing.

"And as Sun Tzu said, 'it is a matter of life and death, a road either to safety or to ruin'. And what makes you think we want revenge, anyway? For what? Have you done something you care to share?" Cole narrowed his eyes, bristling with indignation.

"Ah, you like *The Art of War.* So, you know, 'appear where you are not expected'?"

"What do you want, Chang?" Cole decided to cut through the bullshit.

The older man did not like to be confronted, that was obvious as his sallow skin tightened, wrinkles etched across his forehead. He tugged at his chin whiskers. "I would like the respect due. You asking questions is interfering with my business. Stirring things up. Not necessary. I am just a regular businessman, nothing more. Everybody tell you that."

The false sincerity in the man's tone was cloying and Cole's stomach began roiling with anger. An anger he had to contain as releasing it was a cheap luxury he could ill afford. Chang had Sara. If Cole hadn't known that for certain before, he knew now.

"If you are just a businessman, why are you even here, Chang?" Cole had an idea to further annoy the man, make his visit seem senseless. "Besides, we've already discovered that you're an honest businessman. We intended to give you a pass, anyway."

Chang's eyes hardened with a glint of steeliness, demonstrating his anger was barely under control. Cole had scored a direct hit. "I came today to tell you to save you the trouble of continuing your harassment."

"Asking a few questions in your neighborhood hardly constitutes harassment. But like I said, it's all good." Cole shrugged to demonstrate his indifference, keeping a tight clamp on his emotions. They knew where to look and letting Chang know that would only cause further harm. The brief satisfaction of confronting the man would be offset by the damage of letting him in on it, much as he wanted to grab him by that coiffured hair and beat it the hell out of him.

"You need to keep your word and stay out of Chinatown. Stop sending in cops to do your job," Chang advised, needing to get in the last word.

"Sorry, can't do that. Somebody knows something we need to know."

"What? Maybe I can help?"

"Not if you are just an ordinary businessman. You are not in the information loop. What can you possibly offer us?" Cole scoffed and shook his head, keeping his cards pressed to his chest. No way would he give the man one iota of information.

The man's tell was obvious—he hated being seen as out of the loop. Useless. Made him look small and not the big man of Chinatown fame. *Good, keep the asshole on edge. Best chance to learn something, have him make a mistake.*

"Still, I will let you know if anything unusual happens. Chinatown is my island. My world. Best keep to yours." Chang gestured at his still and silent bookends. "Let's go. We're done here. Nothing else to be learned."

Chang and crew turned on their heels and Cole switched the computer screen back on, using the door security camera to watch the men exit the building and climb into last night's van. He shook his head, unhappy with himself. If he'd been paying attention, he would have seen them arrive and been better prepared. He needed to add a code that would send an alert when someone came through the front door. He thought of the simple low-tech bell solution at Paradise Massage. Had that been just this morning? So much had gone on in the interim, too much really to make it all fit. And the way things stood with Gabby. *God, no, I can't go there right now.*

He set to work, made the quick adjustment to the security system and had just gotten to work when the front door buzzed as it opened. Looking up, he just got a quick flash of Beau coming his way. *Damn it.* Last person he needed or wanted to see right now. Why hadn't he had the decency to wait at the hotel until this was all over?

"Hey, bro." His brother's grating voice trying to sound young and hip set his teeth on edge.

"Morning." He managed the single word with eyes focused on the computer screen.

"Got a sec?"

He groaned, not bothering to hide it. "First Chang, now you. What is it?"

"Who's Chang? Pretty late or early for visiting." Beau ran a hand over his hair. He'd gotten a haircut since Cole seen him last, making him an exact ringer for him. Just great.

Cole glanced at the time on the bottom right of his screen: five-thirteen. The clock ticked all the louder inside his head. Was Sara okay? Was she wide awake as well, staring at the dismal walls of a dingy storage container? Or was she inside a smaller cage? He swallowed the bile that rose in his throat. So young. She must be so frightened. Another thought burned even stronger in his soul, pushed itself to the forefront, escaping its bounds. Was this was had happened to his son? Had Mathew been caged? Left to suffer? *God, no, not now, I can't handle this right now.* His thoughts tumbled, steamrolled through his tired mind, an out-of-control freight train. But, and it was a big but, if he could save Sara, that would count for something, right? Save another parent the anguish of never knowing what happened to their child? Allow some semblance of peace for others, if God found him worthy of taking up the cause? He clung to that hope as he turned to face his brother.

"Chang's just a guy. Not important for you to know. Why are you here now? I've got a ton of work to do."

"I'm sorry. Okay, no need to be a grouch about it, but I just had to see you. There's a lot you don't know — that I couldn't tell you before."

"Fucking great, now I'm the grouchy one." Cole let some of the huge well of anger stored up over years of frustration with his brother vent. Immediately regretted it.

"Look, Cole, I know you got a lot to be upset with me for."

"Ya think."

"But I'm trying here. If you could meet me even a little of the way, this would all be so much easier. Give me a chance to explain." Beau's tone had the ring of sincerity, his eyes filled with pain.

Damn it. Now he was the asshole in the room. But the guy pushed all the wrong buttons.

"Sorry. I'm just worried about a case," he mumbled, fidgeting with his wireless mouse, pretending to concentrate on the computer screen.

"We all have worries, Cole. It's the nature of living."

Sanctimonious prick. Since when did you ever worry about anything except where your next high was coming from? Resentment simmered. He swallowed it down, taking a few deep breaths. He'd read somewhere that was supposed to help. So why wasn't it working?

"Why are you here right now, Beau? Bit early in the morning for you to be out and about isn't it? In fact, how did you even know I was at work?" Rude but effective. Beau had the grace to look caught in the act. So, he'd been in touch with someone else at TETRAD. Silk maybe? She had a soft spot for family.

"Silk told me, if you must know. Said we could have a bit of quiet this morning if I came by. Give us some time to talk."

"So, you knew I was here. You know, if you think I'm ever going to forget what's happened between us, you need your head examined."

"By the way, I've had my head examined lots in the last year. And it does help. Maybe you need to consider it, as well. You're obviously carrying a lot of grief and anger. Not healthy to do that."

"Who are you to tell me what I need to do!" This time, his anger exploded.

"A man who'd fallen into the dark abyss, same as you, and come back. There's light at the end of the tunnel, hope, and I pray you find that out, and soon, brother. You're going to fuck up the rest of your life if you don't. Fuck up every new chance at having a good life."

Cole saw red. It pulsated over his vision, staining the room.

Beau handed him a card. He took it. Tried to read what it said, his hands shaking with the effort to contain himself. It took a few seconds for the few words to make any sense.

When you are ready, we're here to help.

He turned it over and read the address and phone number.

"Call them, Cole. They can help. Set you up with a person to talk out your problems. I guarantee you will gain from the experience. Find a better path."

"I'm on the right path. Helping others is what I do."

"Yeah, but what about you? You've got enough baggage to choke a horse. And I've heard from Silk that there maybe someone new in your life, someone deserving of your best efforts. Do you really want to hurt someone else by being like this? By not being available. You need to give life another chance. If you don't want to take a chance on me, fine. I can handle it. I've been through worse, though I might not like it. I had big hopes coming here that we might set the past behind us. But Silk says this woman's a good person. Hell, she must be, to give a McClintock a chance. And it's never too late, Cole, not unless you're dead and you're a long way from that."

Anger raged hotter, fueled by having his brother talking about him behind his back. Thinking he could come here and talk about his personal shit like this. Like he had any fucking right.

"Don't talk about her like you know her. You know *nothing*, Beauregard, absolutely *nothing* about it." He moved a step closer to his brother, fists clenched at his side. "If you don't shut the fuck up and get out of here *right the fuck now*, I won't be held accountable for my actions."

"If you'll just let me —"

The final straw.

With a bellow of rage, he went for him. He hit his brother with his fist, dead center of his chin. It was a sharp upper cut and snapped Beau's head straight backward. A loud thud resounded over the buzz of angry bees that filled Cole's brain. Beau grunted with pain, flailing his arms about. Crashed into a nearby table setup with an array of supercomputers, sending one of the keyboards flying to the floor, snapping it in half.

It felt damn good, getting that first shot in. Cole wiped the cold sweat from his forehead, assessing the damage. A trickle of blood ran down Beau's chin. He watched his brother, waiting for his move, knowing from long experience he was a damn good fighter. He'd have to keep his guard up.

The two men circled each other, their movements wary. Beau swiped the blood off his chin with his hand, giving a sardonic rise of his eyebrows. His expression spoke volumes.

"That the best you can do, bro?" he asked, displaying some fancy footwork as he avoided the pieces of destroyed technology littering the area around his feet.

"Little out of practice," Cole said with a shrug, his fists raised, watching his twin with care. "But it's all coming back to me now."

Beau launched himself at Cole, grabbing him around the waist, taking him down to the floor with him. They rolled, each trying to get a shot in. A grunt of pain from Cole as Beau dug a sharp elbow into his stomach. A squawk from Beau as Cole shoved him hard against the cement floor.

Cole twisted away, Beau trying to stop him. Got to his feet. *Fucking slippery eel. Just like when he was a kid.* They continued circling each other, warriors looking for an opening, any opportunity. Beau launched himself at Cole, knocking him right off his feet. Cole pounded on Beau's back trying to get him to let go, the thuds echoing in the huge warehouse.

This time, Beau didn't throw a punch, though he could have. Instead, he seemed to be struggling to just stop Cole from doing any more damage.

"You got it out of your system yet or do you need to hit me again?" Beau growled.

"Fuck you! You deserve a lot more. After what you put Mom and Dad through, what you put me through."

Cole rolled on top of him, Beau managing to duck away at the last moment from a punch. "That all you got?" he taunted.

Another punch went wide. Cole's fist hit the floor, missing Beau by mere inches, sending pain snaking up his arm. Cole shook his arm, trying to recover the use of his hand. He slumped to the side, letting up on the tight hold he had on his brother to cradle his arm to his chest.

Beau leaned over onto his hip, grabbing him into a headlock, his mouth close to Cole's ear where he lay prone on the floor.

He began to whisper.

Cole tried to get away, but his twin persisted, continued murmuring until Cole lay quite still, listening to every single word. His eyes grew wide as Beau spoke his full piece, the meaning of the words sinking in, one by one. *Could it be true?*

A sudden lump filled and tightened in the back of Cole's throat, making it difficult to speak, even if he wanted to. Tears welled up. A sob tore out of his chest. *No. No, it can't be. It can't be true. All this time – wasted.*

Beau's tears joined his as the two men lumbered to an embrace. Cole pounded once on Beau's back, not as hard as before, but letting his frustration out. *Damn it all to hell.*

They got to their feet. Cole wiped his face with the back of his hand, swallowing hard. Time to man up. The last few minutes, fighting with his brother, had released some of his pain, made it easier to breathe. And the revelation gave him hope. Maybe there was a future for them? He had to admit, he would have done the same thing as his twin, if called upon.

"Perhaps now you'll consider counseling?" Beau asked, raising an eyebrow, obviously working hard to achieve a lighter tone. His mouth twisted with the effort. Cole watched him swallow hard and it unseated him again. A mist of tears made the room shine and he shook them away.

"Yeah, in your dreams," Cole scoffed to hide his emotions. Real men just don't do stuff like that. *Right?*

"You might want to consider the effect your fucked-up-ness has on those around you. People who might want more from you than you're capable of giving right now. You know, like, Gabby. Just sayin'."

The comment hit Cole square between the eyes. Was that what was going on? Was this it, the opportunity for a beginning for him and Gabby? The thought floored him. Made his head reel even more, if that were even possible.

Perhaps therapy had helped Beau? He did seem better for it, though he could still throw a pretty good left hook. He swallowed hard and pressed his lips tightly together, realizing he had hit a crossroads. *God, I don't think I can live like this anymore. With the pain, the doubts, the guilt, the terrible sense of shame for not being there for my wife and son.* Something else broke in him, realizing he needed to lay his burdens down. That he could carry not carry them alone any longer.

"Okay, when this is all over — when Sara is safe — I'll give it some thought."

Beau looked stunned, as surprised as Cole found himself for saying it. *Maybe I am ready?* At least ready enough to consider it. The pain on Gabby's face this morning when he had rejected her had hurt him to the quick. *I need to learn another way.* "Well, that's good then."

"Not committing to anything." He warned, not wanting to be boxed in.

"Thinking is the start. Get your mind ready, that's the key."

"Okay, fuck, the clock's ticking. I need more than anything to get back to work."

"Crisis is normally when this stuff surfaces, according to my guy. It's when the soul can't handle the pressure anymore and it gets released. It's a good thing, ColeF. It's when you have the opportunity to embrace a change—a good change."

Cole grunted and turned back to the screen, shutting out his brother. But another crack had appeared, whether he liked it or not, letting in some light, making him want to apologize to Gabby. Maybe, just maybe there was a slight chance for a better life.

* * * *

Day Four: 7:23 a.m.

"Fucking men are just so damn predictable," Gabby grumbled as she printed off the series of photos Celine had taken from the night at the Legend Saloon to be delivered to the soon-to-be-ex-wife. She needed to get onto more important work, but the woman was pressing her for them and she felt guilty in holding things up. And a photograph of the crime was worth a thousand words. *Just hand them over and let them do all the dirty work.* After all, she had already been paid and it only took a few minutes. She insisted on being paid up front, less hassle. She hated being used.

What has she been thinking? Thinking it was a good idea to bed someone she worked with? And now she had to face him. Feel like a fool all over again.

Gabby climbed into her car and started the motor, thrusting the reliable second-hand Honda Civic into gear and spun off in the direction of the client's house. She'd picked the beater up for a song when everything had gone south for her and her fucking cheating ex. She needed to drop the incriminating evidence off before heading into to work at TETRAD. Clear the decks.

"Hey, Gabby, I appreciate you getting here so quickly," Ashley said. The woman looked better today than Gabby had ever seen her before. Every other time she had met her she appeared a bit disheveled, her thoughts unfocused. But not today. Today she had the look of a woman on a mission. Maybe the sting had been a boost to her self-confidence? Good, she was glad to help. Women needed all the help they could get in keeping their lives sorted. Maybe it wasn't such a waste of time after all, taking these cases others so enjoyed turned their noses up at?

"Would you like coffee? I just perked some," Ashley offered, sharing a bright smile.

"No, another time. I'm on a case today. Gotta run. But I brought you these." She handed over the brown manila envelope.

"Good, thanks. I appreciate all your effort." Ashley opened the package and glanced at the half-dozen photos, leafing through them. "Yeah, just like I figured. George's bad for bedding every new piece of tail in the office. And now it's come back to sting him in the ass. Good. Fair enough."

"So, you have decided to go through with it?" Last time she'd seen the woman, Ashley had been wavering, wanting to know, not wanting to know, tearing herself up inside. Typical woman shit, thinking it was all her fault. When damn it, it was the man who was cheating on them.

"Oh, yeah, time to get on with the rest of my life. Lots of men out there who don't cheat and I'm going to find me a good one. Make sure of that next time, even if I have to have him trailed to prove it. You'd be available again, right, help me be certain?"

"Sure. But what ever happened to trust? You know, wedding vows that say you will be true to each other forsaking all comers? Like our parents?"

"Cheaters in that generation, too, but it was usually swept under the rug. This generation, we're savvier. Better at spotting the signs, or at least acting on them. And of course, we got more resources. We can afford to leave their cheating asses behind, move on. We don't have to put up with less than."

"Hmm, you sure seem to have gotten your act together. I admire that. You went through a lot."

"Yeah, well, you learn. But that doesn't mean that if the right man didn't come along, I won't be willing to trust again. Woman can't live on bitterness alone. Or at least according to my best friend, Gail."

"Let's keep in touch," Gabby said as she returned the woman's firm handshake. She had enjoyed the exchange, liked the woman's confidence. A confidence she had had a part in restoring.

She climbed back into her Civic, buckled her seatbelt. Time to get to work. A voice was calling to her, the voice of a young woman who needed her help. *Hold on, sweetheart, I'm on my way.*

She strode into the back room when she discovered no one working reception at TETRAD. Her cowgirl boots clicked on the hard floors of the warehouse as she pretended all was well with her world. No point in letting anyone see her sweat.

"Ready to relieve the nightshift?" she asked Cole, eyeing him working away, keeping her expression noncommittal.

"Uh, yeah, I'm about done here." He shut down his computer and got up. "Let's go."

She gave him a sideways glance, noting the deepening shadows under his eyes. "You get any rest? You looked tired."

"I'm fine." The curt words cut as sharp as a well-honed blade.

She said nothing, just hurried outside and climbed into the truck. Going to be a long, long, day.

She sat silent, not giving him the satisfaction of saying anything to relieve the stress as Cole drove them to the stakeout.

If only they could change partners. But no, Silk had said that Jake was insisting the schedule stay in place. He felt they were just about to break the case wide open and wanted his lead team there for the final takedown. *God, please be right, that we're that close to finding her.*

Sitting and watching the back of Chang's where the van was again parked, she wished things were different, but knew that was never going to happen.

"Beau and I talked this morning."

"What?" Cole had caught her by surprise and she removed one ear bud to hear him better, turning her head toward him and giving him a wide-eyed stare.

"Yeah, he says I need to consider seeing someone."

"Who?"

"You know, someone who makes it their living to listen to others yatter on."

"Oh, and what did you say?" Her breathing sped up, thinking how much this admission must be costing him. Maybe he would make peace with his brother now. Help heal some of his wounds. Lord knows she was no help, judging by the way he had high-tailed it this morning.

"Said I'd think about it."

"Well, that's a good start. You've been through so much—more than most people could imagine going through. Talking about it can only help."

"And talking about a fresh start—" Cole hesitated, biting as his bottom lip, his eyes dark with anguish that stirred her more than she was prepared to let on. "Do you think you can give me another chance to make things right between us? I'm sorry about leaving you in the lurch this morning. Really sorry. It was wrong."

"I don't know, Cole. I'm not good at this kind of thing, either. I've seen so many men cheat on their wives, you have no idea. I was just in it for some fun, you know. Scratch an itch." She made the effort to lighten the atmosphere. She hated to see anyone in such mental pain.

"Not all men cheat, Gabby! I never cheated on a woman in my life. I may have my limitations as a partner, but cheating, no, never going to happen. Once you and I start up, that's it. No other woman. Besides, no woman can hold a candle to you, anyway. Why the fuck would I want to look elsewhere?"

The vehemence of his response stunned her. Not to mention the confession.

"Uh, good. But, I don't know, I can't see any kind of future for us. We're ill-suited to be hooked up with anyone. Couple of lone wolves." Visions of the idyllic rural life danced across her vision and she immediately shut it down. *Like that could ever happen.*

"You are not a lone wolf, for heaven's sake. You're a vibrant, amazing woman. And I didn't need to be in your company for more than a short while to see that was the case. Could you at least give me a chance to make this right? Hold off on a final decision until I've sorted myself? We got chemistry, you and I. There's no saying that's not true. Right? The sex this morning. Right off the charts."

He had her there. "Maybe—" Cole was sounding less and less like he needed a therapist, and more like a man in charge of his destiny. Such an about-face was sending her for a loop. An uncomfortable loop. What the hell had he talked about this morning that sent him to this new place?

* * * *

Day Four: 3:20 p.m.

"Shush. Listen, did you hear that? Tommy's talking about moving a package."

Gabby went silent as business became the focus, listening, and concentrating only on the conversation continuing inside the café.

"We need to move it. Today."

"Where?"

"We pick it up and take it to Joe's. He's expecting us. And make damn sure we're not followed. There's been a couple of idiots watching us, white girl with messy golden-brown hair, blue eyes—kind of pretty—and big white guy with too-short dark hair and eyes. Looks like ex-military asshole."

"And if they follow us?"

"Dump it. Don't need any more of this problem. Big man not here, easy for him."

Gabby's breath stilled in her body. A throbbing pain began right behind her eyes, caused by extreme stress. She turned horrified eyes toward Cole. "Oh, my God! They're going to kill her if they see us following. What do we do? They've made us."

"Relax, Gabby, I thought of this happening. I had someone attach a sensor under the van to track it early this morning. They have no idea. The guy was dressed for the part and pretended to be drunk so he could fall, plant the device and get up right next to the van. We'll follow at a safe distance. Too bad they made us, though, but with a care, we'll be able to track them safely."

"Good thinking, but—just a sec, I'm thinking. Yes! I know what to do! Call up TETRAD, I want a full video conference. Right now!"

"You know, they may not be talking about Sara. Don't get your hopes up too high. They might be talking about another package." He turned a cautioning look her way she ignored. "Hell, they could even be setting us up. They've made us, maybe they even suspect we're listening in."

"They have to be talking about her." Gabby pressed her fist to her mouth to keep from letting her emotions spill, trying to clamp down on her fears for the young girl. A pawn in a game. Cruel and unnecessary. And what for, just for the sake of profit? She was beginning to regret her entry into a man's world, if this was all it held. An image filled her mind that she was unable to suppress this time. An image of living in the country with a white picket fence, a golden retriever playing with children in a well-kept yard, a real home to look after that did not involve shit like this. And yet, she was good at this shit, and it needed doing, whether she liked it or not. Besides, the perfect man for her who wanted to live that can kind of life just did not exist in her world. All confessions aside.

Cole brought up the video screen, putting out a high priority, all-call to TETRAD. Jake and Quinn came on-line at once with Silk a few seconds later.

"What you got?" Jake barked.

"Gabby called the conference. She'll tell you what's up."

"Okay, I have an idea of how to fool Chang and his crew about our whereabouts. A decoy. My sister Celine can pass for me, and apparently, Beau can pass for Cole being his identical twin brother." She looked at Cole who confirmed it with a terse nod. "And since we've been made, how about they come here? Beau's in town, at a hotel, and Celine can take off from work. Then we're free to follow the van when it leaves here."

"Brilliant, Gabby. 'When we are near, we must make the enemy believe we are far away; when far away, we must make him believe we are near'," Cole said, punching Beau's cell number. "Beau, I've got a job that needs doing right this exact moment. If you want to prove you're able to be trusted, that you can be still be there for me, head back to TETRAD right now. Wait for Gabby's sister, Celine. She'll meet you there then the pair of you can come to Chinatown and take over for us. We'll wait for you here as long as we can. And don't worry about keeping a low profile. We want you spotted, just don't make it too obvious. Can you do that, Beau?"

"Yes, I'm on it. No problem. Thanks, Cole. It means a lot to me that you'd call in a pinch."

Cole hung up, waiting for confirmation of Celine's involvement from Gabby. He prayed Beau wasn't all smoke and mirrors again, that he would do what was needed for once.

Gabby was busy talking to Celine. "No time to wait. I need you right this minute to go to TETRAD and join with Cole's brother Beau, then come down here to Chinatown. You're going to be our decoy pair so we can be free to maneuver. Don't know how long it will take, but the case may be breaking! Can you do that?"

"Great. Talk later."

"I'm moving us farther away right now then Celine and Beau can move in closer. We'll be able to follow the van with impunity. Great idea, Gabby, I'm impressed. The gang will think we're still here, fool them into thinking we aren't listening in if they suspect it, and we can follow."

She nodded, a wave of intense feeling rushing in, making her aware the worst of the rollercoaster ride was just beginning. Too many unknowns, too many variables to be sure of who knew what, who was fooling who, and who was going to get hurt. Her brain screamed, please, dear God, keep Sara safe. She kept it bottled up as the seconds ticked by, waiting for Celine and Beau to get into position. *Tick tock. Tick tock.*

Twenty-seven gut-wrenching minutes later, the decoy pair pulled into position on Pender Street, a block from the café.

"Now, we're ready," Cole said, the muscles around his mouth strained with tension.

"Good." Gabby nodded.

They waited together silent, tension rising, the minutes and hours slipping away.

"They're on the move!" Cole near shouted in her ear, sitting up straighter in his seat, his sunken eyes lit up with an almost unholy fire as he turned and grabbed her arm.

Gabby shook herself awake. She'd been drifting, the lack of sleep catching up.

The van's tracking device showed it was indeed on the move, leaving the parking spot behind the café. Cole started the truck. They drove down the side street slowly, staying well behind the van, choosing to pull onto Pender Street a few blocks down from the café to avoid detection. Fuck, was this it?

She was wide awake now, her vision riveted on the road ahead.

A hush descended in the cab of the truck that began affecting her breathing as they made their way farther and farther through the heart of Vancouver, on their way to the docks. The ten-minute drive seemed like a lifetime. She struggled to draw a full breath into her lungs. Just stay calm.

Cole's phone rang and he answered over the Bluetooth speaker phone to avoid taking his hands off the wheel as he turned onto Waterfront Road.

"Cole, it's Nils. You alone? I have something important to share."

"You can say whatever it is in front of Gabby. We have no secrets."

"Gabby?"

"Yeah, my new partner at TETRAD. We're working the case together and following a suspect right now. Why are you calling?"

"Okay, I thought about what you said, about it all starting with saving one child, the one right in front of you, and I admit, Sara's plight got to me. You know, if each person just helped one other, the whole world would improve. I want to help you, and I'm sorry I didn't do it earlier. I'm the bearer of good news, buddy. I've got what you need. Only one better. A double sting, a Trojan Horse I've built into the source code. The bastards won't know what hit them when it leads right back to them. Ready to go right now! I know you're almost out of time."

"What! I thought you couldn't do this thing? That it went against your grain? But yeah, great, though I'm still hoping we won't need it. I have news for you, too. It depends on how tonight plays out—the next few minutes are critical—but I think we might have an alternate solution. Bring these guys down before the deadline. In fact, they're maybe leading us right toward her right as we speak."

"That's great! Good luck. I'll catch up later. Stay safe."

"Will do. And thanks again. You may have just saved someone's life if this falls through and we have to go that far."

Tension increased for her as the city blocks flew by the window. Was this it?

"You okay?"

She didn't trust herself to speak, just nodded, clenching her hands so tight together her fingernails dug into the palms. Was she even cut out for this kind of work? Right now, a cheating husband seemed like child's play.

"Don't worry. They have no idea we're on their tail. And Jake and Quinn will be right behind us when it goes down—if it goes down. They're trailing us right now." Cole pointed at his side mirror. Gabby checked and spotted them in the black SUV.

"What if the van's filled with those homemade bombs?" The question was out before she could hold the words back.

"Unlikely they put any back in after the police investigated. Too chancy. Most they'd have is one or two in their possession."

"Not exactly reassuring." Only takes one to kill. "Cole, if we make it out of this alive, I want to say that, yeah, I'm prepared to give it another shot. The sex, wow, it was amazing. Unbelievable, in fact. And if that's supposed to be one of the tests for beginning a relationship, that we passed it. With flying colors."

Cole snuck a glance at her then reached for and grabbed her hand, squeezing it tight. The electricity sparked between them making her feel reassured for the first time since he'd left her bed. "Thanks. That's all I can ask."

The van ahead of them, driving slower now, turned onto the final stretch that yawned like a peninsula out to the sea. The causeway had water surrounding it on three sides, and commercial ships sunk deep in the rich blue water from their heavy loads, looking like lumbering over-size rafts instead of the wonderfully tall sailing ships of decades past. Sailors and merchant men must miss them, she thought, and not for the first time, wishing the century she had been born into had not been so focused on function over style and form.

"You gonna call her father?" she asked, as they kept their careful distance from the van, the tracking device beeping away on the dash further jarring her stretched nerves. She could not imagine how difficult this had to be for Sara's dad. Then she remembered that Cole had been through it and her heart broke for him. Of course, she could give him another chance. Help him heal.

"No, I don't want to raise false hopes. That wouldn't be fair. Soon as we know anything, I'll call Jon. He's going out of his mind with worry, calling and texting a lot. Worried about every little detail. Not unexpected. I get it."

Cole's voice sounded stressed though he was working hard to contain it. Jon had called three times in the past few hours. The deadline was looming. Cole let her hand go while he instructed Siri to make a phone call to Jake in the vehicle shadowing them.

The overcast day had been threatening rain. Now, it began to pour, the water laden clouds dumping their moisture, obscuring their view of the buildings and containers. Gabby's head began to ache in earnest, the wipers thudding back and forth on the windshield pulsing with her pain. She could barely make out the van, parked in front of a low, long building. The two men got out and went in through one of the front doors.

Cole parked, kept the motor running. "Yes, they've gone into a large building that looks as if it houses offices." He turned to her. "Grab those binoculars out of the glove box."

Cole's cell phone rang, the tone one that set her nerves jangling under current circumstances. He set the call to speaker as well so she could listen in.

"Hey, Jon. Yeah, I was going to call you in a sec."

"Cole, I can't wait any longer! We're running out of time. My God, it's Sara we're talking about. I have to go to the police. Right now, or it'll be too late. They moved up the deadline. We've only got until midnight. That's less than two hours away! I'm calling them — right now. Sorry, but I have to do this!" Jon's frantic voice, raw and filled with pain stabbed at Gabby. The anguish of a father came over the line loud and clear.

"No, Jon, don't. Just give me a little bit longer. We've got a solid lead. In fact, we're tracking a van right now that might be leading us to her. And we've got the source code. 'Satoshi' just called. He's perfected it and agreed to help us. He's got it all ready to go in a moment's notice. If Sara's not where we think she is, then we can use it immediately. Make a trade. But this would be better. Catch them unaware. Get her away from them right now. We're tracking them as we speak."

"My God, really? Oh, fuck, I don't know what to do. I'm going out of my fucking mind! Rose is under doctor's care. She's hysterical, Cole, I don't know what to do. What do I do?"

A short silence, then Jon continued, "Okay, I'll give you another hour. But you got to keep me fully informed, tight in the loop. Call soon as you know anything, anything at all. Dear God, please bring her home safely, Cole, I beg you."

"Of course."

Day Four: 10:19 p.m.

Gabby had found what Cole needed. She handed the binoculars over. He adjusted them to his vision and kept them trained on the doorway the men had vanished into.

"They're coming out now carrying some boxes. Damn it, what if that's all this was? Picking up shit for Chang?" Cole sounded pissed off and worried.

"No, they're going back in."

The seconds stretched. Each one an eternity. The eleventh hour loomed.

"There! They've come out another door at the far end of the building near that fleet of containers. I'm going in. I can't see shit from here."

He reached under the seat and pulled out a gun. Tucked it in the waistband of his jeans to keep it dry. Gabby's stomach lurched. Suddenly, it was all too serious.

"We'll go to the other end of the line and check if they come out there," Jake said over the speaker. The black SUV drove past them a few seconds later.

"You wait here," Cole warned.

The truck door opened and he jumped down to the pavement, ignoring the rain that drenched his T-shirt and jeans within a few seconds.

Gabby watched as he hurried forward to the last spot where the gang members had been seen. She made an instant decision, checked her Taser was in her pocket and got out of the truck. The rain pelted her as she ran toward the line of containers housing cargo destined for the big ships docked in the harbor. Was Sara in one of them? Were they being led right to her?

Shivering with the cold and dread, she raced after Cole. She followed him down the row of containers, some rusty from use, rain bouncing off the metal a steady drone of discord. She lost sight of him in the deluge. Wiping the rain from her eyes, hair plastered to her scalp, she blinked repeatedly to be able to see through the waterfall. A heavy squeaky door being forced open sent her in a new direction.

Hurtling around a corner, she caught sight of a door angled open. This had to be it. Her heart racing, her headache long forgotten, she crept forward, her fingers clutching the Taser.

"Let her go!" Cole shouted.

She couldn't stop herself. She ran full-tilt toward the sound, to come to a dead stop just out of sight of the entrance. Gabby held onto the side of the chilly container that loomed many feet above, inching her way forward until she could see in the narrow space between the opening. What she saw froze the blood in her veins.

Cole faced the two men. Tommy had Sara, a gun pressed to her head. The other gang member, the one she knew as Lee, looked ready to charge at Cole, gun out as well. What the fuck to do?

She looked down at the ground, searching for something to use as a diversion. She picked up a heavy rock, stepped back and threw it with all her might at the side of the cargo container. The sound echoed.

"What the fuck! Who's out there?" Tommy shouted from inside the container.

Jake and Quinn came running out of the swamping rain.

"He's inside with Sara. Tommy and Lee. They've got guns," she shouted at them.

Jake and Gabby raced around to the open doorway of the stark, claustrophobic space that kept out most light and stank of untold horrors. Quinn hung back just out of sight, his gun at the ready. The two gangers were now out-numbered. Jake and Gabby stood side-by-side with Cole, stepping up and over the short ridge of metal into the cargo hold. A house undivided. Would that make the gang members even more dangerous? Or would they have the sense to give up?

A siren began screaming, adding to the pandemonium, proclaiming its imminent arrival. Thank God someone had called the police.

"Stay back," Tommy warned, edging around Cole, Sara pressed tight against him, held hostage by an arm around her throat. Her eyes were wide with terror, her skin pasty pale. Gabby's heart squeezed in sympathy. She backed up closer to the doorway, away from the others. *Hang in there, Sara.*

"Let her go," Cole said, using the siren to his advantage. "The police are on the way. You can't get away with this. They'll hunt you down, no matter where you go. Hurting Sara will only make this all end badly for you. Let her go now. I'll say you cooperated. Get you a better deal."

Indecision slackened Tommy's posture. He stopped dragging Sara toward the doorway. The young girl was terrified, the only sound tiny whimpers as he jerked her about like a puppet.

But he had to know he was trapped, right? Didn't mean he'd see reason, though. A trapped animal could be the most dangerous one of all.

Everyone on the team froze as Tommy continued to inch his way with Sara toward the mouth of the container. He was going to get away—no one could take a chance or Sara could get hurt.

A slight noise from outside the container made Gabby swing her head around to discover the source. She caught a glimpse of a shadowy figure of a man dressed all in black with an umbrella held over his head standing in the doorway, making it hard to see who it was.

"What's going on here, Nephew?" Chang's voice echoed as he lifted the edge of the umbrella enough for Gabby to recognize him. He had a gun in his hand. Pointed right at them.

"Uncle Chang! Good you're here. Keep your gun on these bastards," Tommy said, relief clear at the sight of his uncle. "I'll get our collateral safely away. She's our golden ticket, Uncle. Going to make us a lot of money from the big guy in China."

"What's the meaning of all this? Vu said to come here tonight. That something was going down I needed to know about. What's going on? What have you done?"

"I can explain later. We have to go. *Now*, Uncle. No time to tell you everything. But it's important. This is going to make us a lot of money — I promise. Just keep an eye on these assholes until I can get away." Tommy dragged Sara farther toward the doorway as he pleaded his case with his uncle, frustration clear in his voice.

"Explain now, Nephew," Chong's voice went hard as steel in its intensity, his eyes looking to drive black spikes into Tommy's slender frame.

"Uncle, there's no time for this. I'm family — your nephew. Just help now, please. It's a good thing, I promise, good for everyone. You'll be pleased. You have my word on it."

"No, explain first." Chang shook his head, keeping his gun held steady, still pointed right at the TETRAD crew.

The mask dropped, Tommy's expression changing as though wiped with a sponge.

"Fuck, old man, you need to drop the act, get with the twenty-first century world. It's not about being so careful. You're out of touch. Obsolete. It's foolish to think the modern world wouldn't catch up with you. With all of us. And you let it happen!" Tommy was angry now, his words biting into the older man who froze like a statue at the bitterness spilling out, enduring the cruel lashing. "Your time is past, Uncle. But help me and you can still save face and we can all make money. No one else needs to know. I can make you look good." His voice became wheedling, his tone whiney. *Self-entitled.*

Gabby's breath froze. What next? Would Chang throw in his lot with Tommy? Would he still side with him? The guy was a gangster. Had his finger in a lot of illegal enterprises.

The old man seemed to age a decade right before her eyes as he took in the depth of the betrayal. The gun trembled in his hand. His face paled for a split second and he almost looked lost. Gabby found herself sympathetic. She squelched it, he had many other crimes to atone for. Chang gathered himself, then, drew himself up taller.

"I work for clan. For family. You know nothing of honor. Nothing!" Bitterness exploded from Chang with his words. "How could you betray your family like this? Exposing us to this shit! Don't you realize what you've done? The depth of harm you have now brought onto the Chang dynasty? You've wiped out decades of advancement for us. Brought dark times because of this deed. But it's not too late. Confucius say, 'be not ashamed of mistakes, and thus make them crimes'. There is still time to make this right, nephew. Let the girl go. We are not kidnappers. We don't harm women in this way. We bring them to Canada for a chance at a better life, once they pay off their passage. That is only right. We are not a charity, but a business. We do much good."

"Fuck Confucius and all his stupid sayings!" Tommy's nostrils flared with disgust.

"He's right, Tommy. Give it up now and we can talk about this. Work out a deal. You can help us catch this big guy, your connection, the man safe in China expecting you to do his dirty work for him here. Testify against him. It would go a long way to reducing a sentence—you might even get probation. What do you say? Can we sit down and talk? Like gentlemen? Keep your family from facing further disgrace?" Cole interjected, his tone of voice low and reassuring. A feat Gabby doubted she was capable of at the moment. The sight of Sara in her tattered and dirty prom dress, the stained mattress on the floor, the sad remnants of rotting food and neglect sickened her.

Tommy's expression hardened further, sparks blazing from his dark eyes, his hand tightening around Sara's throat. The girl's face paled as she wiggled within his grasp, grabbing at the arm restricting her airway. Gabby swallowed, trying to dislodge the fear growing in her throat.

"There's nothing to talk about. I'm taking her and leaving, with or without your help, Uncle. Think I need you? Big man will make things right. Bigger man than you. You'll see."

Hang in there, Sara.

As if she heard Gabby's silent entreaty the girl stopped struggling, some focus visible in her eyes once more. Good. She needed to be ready. They could not allow Tommy to move her to another location. She would be murdered for certain.

Chang turned the gun on his nephew. "Let her go. Man is right. We'll sit and talk. Nothing to be gained by further resistance, Nephew. Only harm."

"Fuck—*no*! Back off!" Tommy swung his gun around in a wild arc. Lee, looking uncertain, hovered behind him. He appeared a lesser threat, a henchman following orders only, unable to decide his next move on his own. Gabby's throat constricted, the lump growing in the back of her throat, her heart hammering. She was no longer shivering, her skin blazing with surplus heat from the fearful adrenaline rush exploding within.

Gabby glanced at Cole. He gave her a small nod. *Be ready.*

Tommy dragged Sara the last few feet, her eyes round with fear.

Everything happened at once. Chang launched himself at his nephew, taking him by surprise. Taking everyone by surprise.

Tommy's gun fired, the sound deafening in the confined space.

Chang fell back, dropping to the ground. Tommy threw himself from the container, tripping on the rough edge of the metal doorway, Sara attached to him like a skydiver as they fell in tandem. Without thinking, Gabby launched herself at Tommy, falling onto him and Sara on the ground. The gun fired a second time. She fought tooth and nail, trying to force Tommy to give up Sara. To let go.

Who's screaming?

She rolled on the ground in the wet grass and mud with the pair, struggling desperately to dislodge Sara from Tommy. Rocks bit into her back from the rough terrain. A slug from Tommy across her cheekbone stung like hell. Another one glanced off her forehead temporarily blinding her in one eye. She thrust her hands upwards, pushing Sara away from Tommy, wanting a clear shot at striking him.

He kept twisting away, making it hard to disable him. He knocked the breath clear out of her with a hard punch in her side, making her gasp in pain. She tightened her resolve, pushing the jarring discomfort aside. No fucking way was she ever going to stop trying. *He'll have to kill me first.*

Gabby tried to jab her fingers into his eye sockets to blind him, the action going wide. A second stab hit the target. Dead-on.

The gun flew from his hands, landing on the ground. A third shot zinged by her so close she felt its deadly kiss.

Then other hands were helping, pulling her off Tommy. Someone took Sara away. Cole grabbed her, holding her tightly in his arms. "Are you hit? Are you okay?" He wiped some blood away from the cut above her eye with the bottom of his T-shirt he'd tugged out from his jeans, his touch tender. She winced from the sting.

"I'm fine." Damn, now he was going to complain about her lack of following proper procedure. The thought made her angry and her body betrayed her anger making her stiffen in Cole's arms. He shook her to get her full attention.

"My God, Gabby, you could have been killed!" The look of anguish on his face confused her, draining her anger away in seconds. He pulled her in tight against him, lacing his fingers against her back. His heart was beating so fast she could feel it pulsing against the side of her face as he held her. It gave her pause as she took it its meaning. He did care. The thought filled her with a new sensation. *One of wonder.*

"I'm okay, really, Cole," she whispered, feeling safe held against his broad chest.

"Thank God," he breathed into her hair, squeezing her tighter.

Then she remembered where they were. It wasn't just about them right now.

"How's Sara?" She looked around frantically. Sara was being reassured by Jake, his arms around the crying girl. Quinn had Tommy in his grasp, arms twisted together behind his back, handcuffs being snapped on.

"She's unharmed. She's okay. Thanks to you." Cole pulled her back tight against him again, not letting her go. "Thank God, you're okay. I don't know what I would do if something happened to you." She heard the catch in his tone and looked up into his eyes. Real worry for her safety shone down upon her. Something else, too. She couldn't say for sure what it was. Maybe something to build upon? *A glimmer of hope.*

She looked around, assessing the situation. Chang had been shot in the arm, but was functioning. The man's shoulders drooped with resignation as he held his limb cradled against his chest, blood dripping onto the rough rusted corrugated floor of the cargo container.

Gabby joined Jake, taking over, offering small reassuring sounds as she placed her arms around the shivering girl.

He gave her a curt nod. "I need to speak with you. Now."

Oh, crap. Now, she was in for it.

Gabby dutifully followed Jake a few yards away. Words spilled out of her. "I'm sorry, I didn't think, I just wanted to save her I know that if they'd taken Sara away from here—"

"Does that excuse that you might have gotten yourself killed? Or someone else? Damn it, we're professionals here. There are policies and procedures in place for a reason, Gabby." Jake ran a hand through his hair. "That being said, good work."

She stood there stunned.

"We need people like you at TETRAD. And if you can keep from acting like a maverick in the future, we'd like you to join with us."

His words of approval sent a surge of pride racing through her, chasing away some of the worry of the past few minutes and lessening the physical strain of days of too little sleep and not enough food.

She nodded at Jake, her emotions threatening to overwhelm her. Sara was safe. No one was going to die. It was over. She took a deep breath. *Thank you, God.*

"I would like that very much. You stand for everything I want to represent. Thanks, Jake. I won't let you down."

"Good. Welcome aboard."

Jake turned to assist Quinn then handcuffed Lee. The two gang members were sullen and silent, looking far younger as the aggression deserted them.

Gabby hugged Sara. "It's all over, sweetheart," she murmured. "You're safe now."

Cole made the call. "Jon, we've got someone who wants to speak to you." He handed his cell phone to his daughter.

She grabbed it like it was a lifeline. "Daddy! It's Sara. I'm okay."

Cole and Gabby stood back as she reconnected with her father. "I thought I told you to stay in the truck?" he said, tucking the drenched hair back from her streaming face. "You are a bit of a mess, aren't you?"

His voice shook as he rubbed a smudge of dirt off her unhurt cheek.

"I had to be sure you were safe. Provide backup. Just like you would do for me."

The new tenderness in his eyes made her life expand.

"We'll talk about this later. Set some ground rules."

"Whatever you say, handsome." Her mood was too buoyant to be offended. Turned out, this work was right for her, after all. To make such a difference, to help another person, it felt unbelievable. And she could see in Cole's eyes it was healing him as well. It could be a fresh start. *Please, please let it be so.*

Chang moved closer to the pair, his expression resigned. He bowed. "I am sorry for the actions of my nephew. He has brought shame on the Chang clan. Please accept my humble apologies." He bowed deeper, wincing at the pain in his arm.

Cole gave him a nod, frowning. "We need to get that wound seen to. It's obvious you weren't involved with this thing. But your role modeling sucks. Tommy only did what he did because of the family connections. You bear much of the guilt."

"This is true. But it is said, 'a man living without conflicts, it is as if he never lives at all'."

"'What you do not want done to yourself, do not do to others'," Cole shot back. "You need to step up now. Do the right thing, Chang. It's the only way to save your family from ruin."

Chang pursed his lips as if eating a sour lemon. "You know Confucius. But in life we are called to our purpose with whatever we have to offer. The East thinks different than the West. Sees the bigger picture, allows us to accept our lot."

"Maybe, but you can still keep a moral compass. Find a better way."

Chang shrugged, looking unconvinced, but listening with his head lowered.

"And I don't think the authorities will give you much choice. If you don't testify against your nephew, you may be booked as an accomplice. Stands to reason. He did all this in your employ and you did nothing to intervene until now. When it was almost too late." Cole's voice turned sharp, he had to be thinking of how it could have turned out, if luck had turned against them.

"My dad wants to speak to you, Mr. McClintock," Sara said, interrupting the exchange, holding out the cell phone.

Cole took it from her outstretched hand and pressed it to his ear.

"Cole. My God, thank you! You've saved my baby. I can never thank you enough. Whatever you need, just ask. I owe you. More than you can know."

"Do you know anyone in the movie business? I got a young waitress who could really use a break," Cole said with a shaky laugh. "And a massage parlor worker I owe big-time who wants more gifts to give her friends or to sell on for herself."

Gabby watched him, saw him swallow hard, tears misting his eyes as he listened to his friend speak. The pain of his own experience was bared, had to be. Remembering. Cole had never had this happen—his child had never been returned to him. And most likely never would be. Abducted children were seldom seen again when a stranger took them. The harsh truth made Gabby's eyes well up further. She turned away, took a few deep breaths. The odor of fresh rain on earthen ground steadied her, cleared her aching head. She tried to focus on what would be happening next. There would be hours of grueling questioning, no doubt. She would need all her strength and a full gallon of coffee. What she wouldn't give for a shower, but that would have to wait.

She listened to Cole reassure his friend, the cost of his generosity far higher than anyone could know. *Humans have it hard. They have to experience something to truly understand.* Her thoughts squeezed, wanting to help ease his sorrow, as close to understanding his pain as was possible. *Please, please let saving Sara give him some ease*, she prayed with all her might. Cole had been through more than most people could ever imagine having to bear, except perhaps, in the midnight hour when thoughts can send fear into the hearts of the bravest people that they cannot always keep their loved ones safe from harm. She forced herself to give up the grim thoughts, reminding herself that Sara was safe. That goodness and light had won this day. One day at a time. The old words mattered. Chang knew that. She admired some of his life philosophy while abhorring his business practices. He was right about conflict, though. *It resides in all of us. And each day we begin again. Time to begin anew.*

The sirens drew closer and the moment of extreme introspection for Gabby passed. Policemen and ambulance personnel took over the crime scene, going about their tasks with brutal efficiency, bagging evidence for later. The two bullet casings were found, blood splatter evidence collected.

A sudden shout broke through the efficient and calm actions of the professionals cleaning up the crime scene. It drew Gabby's quick attention, swinging her head around to see what was going on. Celine came into sight between two of the cargo containers. She began running and knocked right into Gabby, Beau following close behind. Celine threw her arms around her, her expression a mix of emotions making it obvious the past few hours had taken their toll on her. "Thank God you're safe!"

Celine hugged her so hard she squeezed all the breath from her body, making her wince at the immediate pain in her side.

"You okay?" Celine asked.

"Yeah, I'm fine now. You must be Beau." Gabby extended a hand to Cole's brother. They did indeed look alike, but Gabby could see small differences, checking out the handsome mug that mirrored Cole's own. "Thanks for your help," she added, giving him a grateful nod.

The TETRAD crew stood together, their job completed, waiting, knowing the next few hours they would be inundated with questions. Gabby stood right in the center of the far taller, stronger group of males. But she was not intimidated. She'd earned her right to be there among them. Somehow, she would dig down and find the strength within to get through the next few hours. Then sleep for days.

Jake's cell phone rang. "Yeah," he said, not leaving his crew alone.

A pause as Jake listened, his face darkening by the second with whatever was being said by the caller.

"Fuck! Hard to believe there are such monsters in the world. Yes, I think I can convince my partners that this needs their immediate attention. ASAP. We're just finishing a case and we'll be free in a few hours. Good. Yes. We'll talk later."

Jake slipped the phone back in his pocket. He now had everyone's rapt attention, no doubt about it.

"Our skills are needed. Dark web shit involving a child pornographer ring that's gone global with ties to a guy calling himself Lord Satan."

If there was a worse kind of human excrement than that kind of low life, she didn't know what it was. Yes, rest could always come later. The mission to help the innocent and take down the scumbags always came first. *I'm ready.*

* * * *

Six months later

A hush descended over the congregation as the pipe organ's two thousand, eight hundred and ninety-nine pipes stilled, the last melodic notes drifting away in the morning sun glinting through the stained-glass windows of Our Lady of the Holy Rosary Cathedral in downtown Vancouver. The wedding ceremony followed the service in perfect harmony, Gabby's attention drifting in and out as if in a dream. She stood beside her man who looked so handsome, well shaven and dressed in a white shirt and black suit. The fragrances of sweet lilac and lily-of-the-valley blossoms drifted up from her cascading bouquet, adding a powerful sense of otherworldliness. She handed the flowers to Celine who stood on her other side, gorgeous in a mauve chiffon gown.

"Do you take this man to be your husband, to love and to cherish until death do you part?"

Gabby gazed into Cole's chocolate-colored eyes that housed no pain, but only a forever love. It flowed into her, settling her nerves. The past six months had been a rollercoaster of emotion as they had come together, sorted out their differences and cemented their relationship. Though he had more to work out then she did, still, she had a new-found belief in the sanctity of man and woman. That they could build a life together, she had no doubt. She knew she was giving back the same faith in her own loving gaze as she prepared to speak the words that bound.

"I do," she said, the conviction clear behind her words. An all-star cast stood behind them, supporting them, cheering them on. His best man and brother Beau, Celine, her maid of honor, Silk, Sara and Rose rounding out her bridesmaids while Jake, Quinn, Jon and Nils did duties for Cole.

He smiled, a small tear escaping.

"I do. And I further promise to love and cherish you and build you that white picket fence you always go on about. And get our future children that golden retriever. But moving to the country, afraid that's out for now. You'll have to settle for a cottage at the lake in the summer."

She swallowed the lump in her throat that his words brought forth, giving a shaky chuckle that ended with a soft hiccup.

"You may now kiss your bride."

The healed man she saw before her bent his head and captured her lips with his own. The difficult journey of intensive therapy behind them, they could now begin their life together. It made her even more proud to be standing up before witnesses, declaring their love. Then he dipped her down for a longer kiss, taking her by surprise, rustling the fabric of her tulle and white satin gown, making her lace veil flow out all around her in a soft sign of contentment. Life with Cole was going to be wonderful beyond all her imaginings. She just knew. Sure, there would be difficulties. Whose life did not include them? But with Cole, she'd be able to navigate them, find a solution for their own personal team of Banks and McClintock.

"I love you, beautiful," he whispered in her ear, his hot breath tantalizing her neck, sending thrills racing through her, warming her to the depths of her soul. Their red-hot lust for each other had not abated, only grown deeper and stronger with each passing day.

"I love you, handsome. More than I can say."

Bells high overhead began to sway and peel, their clappers striking all eight tuneful octaves in the high-spiraled loft of the cathedral's gothic tower as they sang of joy and life. Each ringing note of celebration seeming to agree with all the congratulations being expressed by friends and family. A strong chorus of good wishes that announced the beginning of their new lives together. And a fresh chance at happiness. What more could a gal ask for?

It was just about time to exit for their honeymoon in Hawaii when Gabby looked up to see her sister, Celine, listing sideways, almost stumbling across the floor in the direction of the ladies' room. And who was grinning and moving along in the same direction right behind her, but Cole's brother, Beau. *Oh, oh.* Oh, well…

Want to see more from this author?
Here's a taster for you to enjoy!

The TETRAD Group:
Racing the Whirlwind
January Bain

Excerpt

"Whoever fights monsters should see to it that in the process he does not become a monster.
And if you gaze long enough into an abyss, the abyss will gaze back into you." – Friedrich Nietzsche

Alysia Rossini peered through the windshield of her Dodge RAM at the weather, which was growing fouler by the second. Her hands were clamped so tight to the steering wheel that her knuckles ached. The painted lines delineating the watery pavement had long vanished. Desperate to keep the vehicle on the road, she leaned in closer to the dash, her clothes damp and clammy from the perspiration that trickled down her spine. She had the wipers cranked to their highest setting, yet they were unable to keep up with the deluge of sleeting rain lashing the thick glass in heavy gusts. Her stomach churned with worry and the terrible sense of foreboding disquiet that had crept in during the hour-long journey, fueled by her intense isolation.

The hazy, gray, uncaring Cascade Mountains stretched out for hundreds of kilometers in all directions, looking like a distant planet. Driving home alone made Alysia hesitant to pull over. It was just as easy to get rear-ended on this treacherous highway as not. And that vehicle following behind was stalking too damn close. The driver needed their fucking head examined.

A few more tense kilometers inched by, Alysia clenching her hands tight to the wheel and flicking her glance at the rear-view mirror every few seconds. Her reduced speed kept her from hydroplaning the four-wheel-drive truck but increased the length of time with the idiot on her tail.

Finally, the squall began to ease, the lights of the vehicle behind her becoming more than just two white eyes glaring through the mist. Rolling her head from side to side, she worked to loosen the tenseness of her shoulders. The harsh reality of her twenty-four-hour work day followed by a visit with her friend Kate flashed through her mind, bringing with it added sadness and desperation — and an even more acute sense of isolation.

She shook her head, trying to shake the memories free. Reliving a nightmare loop never solved a damn thing. What she needed most was a drink. Ease from the pain of the job and Kate's devastating illness. Thank goodness it wasn't far to the gas station. She sped up, pressing her foot down on the pedal. The lights of the forecourt beckoned just ahead, sanctuary in a storm.

Oh, God no. The SUV following too damn close fishtailed in her rear-view mirror. It swayed side to side in a macabre dance, jerking back and forth like an artful pickpocket escaping the hands of justice. In slow motion, Alysia took in the horror of the vehicle beginning its death roll. It spun out of control, end over end, then came to rest on the side of the highway, belching billows of smoke.

She took her foot off the gas and swung the wheel to the right, preparing to turn around and pull to the side of the road near the stricken vehicle. No point in her having an accident as well.

She thrust her truck into park, glancing at the SUV ahead of her. Steam poured from the wreck in undulating waves. The wheels still spun, their fancy chrome hubcaps catching glimmers of light from her fog lamps.

Picking up her cell phone, she made the call.

"Nine-one-one, how may I help?" a voice on the other end of the lifeline asked in a calm, reassuring manner.

"Be advised there's a single vehicle accident on the Coquihalla, just north of the Great Bear snow sled, and five hundred meters south of the service station. I'm Alysia Rossini, trauma nurse with BC-STAR. The only one on scene. Vehicle rolled over about thirty seconds ago. Please call my crew and alert them to land in the parking lot at the gas station. Oh, and to watch for the overhead wires on the north side of the lot."

She glanced up again, a strange popping sound pulling her attention away from the operator recording her call. "Advise the vehicle's now on fire! I'm heading in!" She cut the call and thrust the phone into her jacket pocket. More help was on the way, but it wouldn't be for at least fifteen or twenty minutes. That was, if they could fly in this poor weather.

After grabbing a fire extinguisher and her portable trauma bag — a smaller version of her work kit — from the seat behind her, she opened the driver's door, stepping out onto the slippery roadway. Freezing rain pelted her head and shoulders, each stinging piece of water a harsh rebuke she took scant note of. The sight of flames emerging from near the front of the vehicle sent her adrenaline skyrocketing. She swallowed hard, focused on the next few precious moments of opportunity to save a human life from being snuffed out of existence.

She raced to the overturned SUV, her move second nature. Only tonight there was no secondary nurse running alongside her from the helicopter to the scene. She would be the only one providing the critical first few moments of assistance — often the difference between life and death.

She dropped her kit a few feet from the vehicle but held on to the fire extinguisher. Pulling off the metal firing pin, she directed the heavy red cannister's black hose at the undercarriage near the motor compartment, where bluish streaks of flame fueled by gasoline and rubber were shooting out and already rising higher.

How many people involved? She'd only seen the driver's head illuminated by dashboard lights, but that didn't mean there couldn't be others. *Please, please don't let there be children.* That was the worst. Innocent victims forever haunted their rescuers.

She took deep breaths to steady herself, taking in air permeated with the stench of burning oil and plastic. The dry chemical cloud meant to kill the flames only added to the stink, making her head ache.

She fought the flames, smothering them until nothing but dark smoke rolled off the wreck. The night became silent with the crackle of fire gone. No screams. Was the driver unconscious? *Or dead?*

She threw the empty container away and grabbed her emergency bag, dragging it closer on the freezing roadway. On her hands and knees, cold and wet seeping through her jeans, she approached the driver's door. Peering through the glass, she used her hand to swipe away the accumulated moisture. A man hung upside down from his seat, safety harness still in place, air bags deployed. No movement. She grabbed her flashlight from her kit and directed it inside. Just the one person. *Thank you, God.*

She reached for the door handle and tried jerking it open to find it stuck, hard.

"Damn it!" The expletive lowered her stress somewhat. A crowbar's image flashed into her brain. She raced back to her truck and located the one under the front seat. After racing back to the wreck, she slipped the tool into the crack between the door and the side panel and pried with all her might.

"Jaws of life would be handy right now," she muttered. She put her whole body into the action, all hundred and twenty-five pounds of sinew and muscle. She never neglected working out. Her job required a fit body. Unfortunately, she took most things to excess. A sudden memory of abusing alcohol at a convention the week before made her wince. Okay, so every responder on her crew had done the same, but she had to get a lid on things before her life spiraled right out of control.

The door gave way under her continued onslaught. Creaking in protest, it opened enough that she could squeeze her way inside. She placed her fingers on the man's neck, checking for a pulse. *Just detectable.* He was struggling, gasping for breath. Blood dripped from a large gaping cut on his forehead, accounting for his unconscious state. She needed to get oxygen into his system, fast.

"Are you okay?" she asked, trying to wake him. He looked to be in his late twenties or early thirties, close to her age, maybe a bit older, with curly dark hair that flopped over his eyes. He looked somewhat familiar, but she couldn't place him.

No response.

She didn't want to move him, not until help arrived and they could safely secure him to a backboard. That was one of the things she didn't carry. If there were unseen internal injuries or spinal fractures, she could do more damage. His body had been badly abused.

The harsh breathing stopped and her adrenaline spiked. *Cardiac arrest?*

She had to incubate him or he was at risk of brain damage. She moved away and opened her medical kit, pulling out a laryngoscope to locate his vocal cords, the entrance to his trachea. The bag also included the polyvinyl endotracheal tube with a balloon at the end required for the delicate operation. She needed to create a seal to prevent air from leaking out when she forced a breath with the portable suction bag, and to stop the patient from vomiting. It would be a tragedy to be saved, only to die of aspiration pneumonia days or weeks later.

Working upside down, all by herself, was going to make it challenging, if not impossible. But it wouldn't be the first time she'd had to jury-rig a device to work in the patient's favor. In the field, a nurse lived by her wits and quick ability to figure out what was necessary, or she washed out and left the profession for calmer waters.

Minutes slipped by. Alysia struggled to tube him, normally a two-person job. But then the hose cooperated and slipped down his trachea and into place. He was bagged. *Thank you, God.*

She began the process of getting life-giving air to his lungs. In and out. In and out. *Just breathe, that's it.*

How long until help arrives? BC-STAR air prided itself on lift-off being within five minutes of getting the call. No vehicles had gone by and no one had left the gas station to check. The fire couldn't have been large enough to be seen from that distance.

She looked into the man's face again, brushing back his wet hair to check the deep wound on his forehead that showed the white of bone. It dripped a steady stream of blood, almost black in the low light.

Who was he? The shape of his face haunted her. She was becoming more positive she knew the guy.

Then his eyes opened. Eyes that had haunted her since she was twelve years old stared back at her.

Oh. My. God. Time jerked to a punishing halt.

Not him.

Not the monster who had murdered her entire family. In cold blood. She wanted to yank the device out of his evil throat, to use it to strangle the life right out of him. Her hands froze in their self-appointed task. Her heart stuttered and her breathing grew harsh, forcing its way in strangled gasps from her horrified chest.

Was he stalking her? Was that why he'd been following so close behind her? No one would know if she just let him go into the good night, ended it right here and now. She could. She knew how. She had the means. Could anyone really blame her?

The police hadn't believed her all those years ago — said he'd had an airtight alibi in being away at that Ivy League school his parents had sent him to, to correct his behavior, to make better use of his intellect that tested right off the charts. But Alysia had always known he'd gotten away with murder, had taken revenge on her family for perceived harm to his own — a perception that had later proven unfounded.

And now he was back. At her mercy.

They stared at each other for a timeless moment. His eyes dark pools of emptiness, he gave no quarter. The decision was hers.

The roar of the helicopter engine overhead alerted her to incoming. She still had a couple of minutes yet — they had to get to the scene from the parking lot. There was still time to let the bastard die.

The staring contest continued for a few more deadly seconds. Her hand hesitated on the tube, wanting to yank it out. *Administer no aid. End it.* It wouldn't take much. Just hold her hand over his mouth and nose until all breathing ceased. His injuries would explain it.

The dilemma sliced into her brain. Pain followed. Her head felt about to explode with the acute stress. Her throat tightened. *No winning on this one.* Let him die — she lost. Let him live — she lost…

Home of Erotic Romance

Sign up for our newsletter and find out about all our romance book releases, eBook sales and promotions, sneak peeks and FREE romance books!

About the Author

January Bain has wished on every falling star, every blown-out birthday candle and every coin thrown in a fountain to be a storyteller. To share the tales of high adventure, mysteries, and full-blown thrillers she has dreamed of all her life. The story you now have in your hands is the compilation of a lot of things manifesting itself for this special series. Hundreds of hours spent researching the unusual and the mundane have come together to create a series that features strong women who don't take life too seriously, wild adventures full of twists and unforeseen turns, and hot complicated men who aren't afraid to take risks. She can only hope the stories of her beloved Brass Ringers will capture your imagination as much as they did hers when she wrote them.

If you are looking for January Bain, you can find her hard at work every morning without fail in her office with two furry babies trying to prove who does a better job of guarding the doorway. And, of course, she's married to the most romantic man! Who once famously replied to her inquiry about buying fresh flowers for their home every week, "Give me one good reason why not?" Leaving her speechless and knocking her head against the proverbial wall for being so darn foolish. She loves flowers.

January loves to hear from readers. You can find her contact information, website details and author profile page at https://www.totallybound.com